NIGHT ON TERROR ISLAND

PHILIP CAVENEY

ANDERSEN PRESS · LONDON

First published in 2011 by
Andersen Press Limited,
20 Vauxhall Bridge Road,
London SW1V 2SA
www.andersenpress.co.uk
Reprinted 2011

The right of Philip Caveney to be identified as the author
of this work has been asserted by him in accordance with
the Copyright, Designs and Patents Act, 1988.

British Library Cataloguing in Publication Data available

ISBN 978 1 84939 270 9

Typeset by FiSH Books, Enfield, Middx.
Printed and bound by CPI Group (UK) Ltd, Croydon, CR0 4YY

CHAPTER ONE

THE PARAMOUNT PICTURE PALACE

Kip McCall let himself out of the house and walked into the village. It was a warm Friday evening in July and school was out for the summer. He stood for a moment, looking up at the Paramount Picture Palace, thinking how much he loved it and how lucky he was that his dad owned a cinema. Not that Dad ever looked at it that way. He was forever telling Kip how difficult it was to make ends meet and that he might not be able to keep the old place running much longer.

Mind you, he'd been saying that for as long as Kip could remember.

The Paramount was a scruffy, single-screen cinema, one of the last of its kind in an age when multiplexes ruled the earth. It had been built back in the 1920s by Dad's great-grandfather and had been in the McCall family ever since. These days it was looking pretty ropey. The front of the building was badly in need of a paint job and there were several tiles missing from the walls, but Kip couldn't have been prouder if it had been built from twenty-two carat gold.

1

Ever since he was old enough to walk and talk, he'd spent most of his spare time at the Paramount, helping his dad run things. Maybe that was why he was so mad about films. He didn't think he was exactly a geek, though plenty of people had accused him of being one, he just loved to watch movies, and when he wasn't watching them, he was reading about them, or talking about them, or looking forward to seeing the next one. So it was fortunate that Dad owned the cinema because it meant that during the holidays, and most weekends, he got to help out there and see all the films for free.

He'd always imagined that one day the Paramount would be his. But he realised now how unlikely that was. Dad was always talking gloomily about the coming of digital films and how, when that happened, it would all be over for the Paramount. A digital projector cost something like fifty thousand pounds, Dad said, money he simply didn't have, and besides, the tiny projection room over the front entrance wouldn't be big enough to house the equipment, so, at best, they had a few years left of struggling along, doing it the old-fashioned way.

Kip looked up at the shiny black letters clipped to the board above the entrance. PUBLIC ENEMY NUMBER ONE; a brand-new film for the start of a brand-new week. Kip had been looking forward to this one; the reviews had been excellent.

2

He went in through the entrance doors and found Dad sitting in the ticket office. He was going through a stack of paperwork, pausing every now and then to shake his head.

'How's it looking?' asked Kip. As usual, the paperwork seemed to consist of unpaid bills.

'Not good,' said Dad gloomily. 'We didn't break even last week.'

'They'll come flooding in for this new one,' Kip assured him. 'It's got Russell Raven in it. His films always do well.'

'Can't do any worse than *Love Reigns*,' said Dad, referring to the film they'd had last week. 'I can't understand it; it had Oscar nominations and everything.'

Kip frowned. He'd tried to talk Dad out of booking that one. It had been unbelievably soppy, a costume drama about young Queen Victoria and her romance with Prince Albert. On Tuesday night, they'd had exactly six people in to watch it. Kip felt fairly confident that *Public Enemy Number One* would do better as, judging by the trailer, it featured some of his favourite things – action, suspense, car chases and big explosions.

'Any news about a replacement for Norman?' asked Kip.

Norman was the Paramount's projectionist. He didn't go back to the 1920s or anything, but he had certainly been there for fifty years. He hadn't been in the best of health lately and last week he'd announced that he had decided to retire to his sister's house in Alderly Edge and that he was giving notice of one week.

This was the worst news they could have had. Dad knew a little bit about projecting films, but not enough to cope if some problem arose, something that seemed to happen every other night. So Dad had put a frantic advert in the *Manchester Evening News*, hoping that there would be somebody out there who could help him. For five days there had been nothing and it was beginning to look as though they were in real trouble, but now Dad was handing Kip a letter.

'That was pushed under the door when I came in,' he said. 'What do you make of it?'

It was written in black ink in a weird, squirly kind of writing, the kind of thing you just didn't see any more. Kip read it with interest.

Dear Mr McCall

I read of your recent predicament in the Evening News. *No cinema can afford to be without a projectionist. Fortunately, I am a master of the profession, and have worked at cinemas all over the world, including Il Fantoccini in Venice. I would be interested in the advertised post and shall call upon you soon, to offer my services.*

Yours sincerely
Mr Lazarus

Kip looked at his dad, then turned the letter over, wondering if there was anything else. 'There's no address or phone number,' he noted. 'Mr Lazarus. Cool name. And what's this Il Fanto-wotsit?'

'Il Fantoccini,' said Dad helpfully. He shrugged his shoulders. 'Search me. A cinema, I suppose.'

'We'll Google it when we get home,' suggested Kip.

Dad dropped the letter onto his desk. 'Who writes a letter and doesn't leave an address or a phone number?' he muttered.

'Or an email address,' added Kip.

'Exactly.' Dad glanced at his watch. 'Maybe you'd better get the popcorn on; it's seven-thirty.'

CHAPTER TWO

MR LAZARUS

Kip went into the confectionary booth. He switched on the popcorn machine and opened a huge bag of corn kernels.

'I suppose your girlfriend will be in tonight?' Dad shouted through.

Kip winced. Dad was talking about Beth, but as usual he'd got it all wrong. Beth was just his mate from school. She was as mad about movies as Kip was and she always came in on a Friday to watch the new release. Dad never charged her for a ticket because he seemed to think there was something funny going on, but it wasn't like that. Kip and Beth were just pals but it was pointless telling Dad that. He was always winking and pulling funny faces.

'There'll be three of you tonight,' Dad told him. 'Your mum phoned to say she's dropping Rose off.'

'Aww, Dad!' protested Kip. 'That's not fair.' Rose was Kip's little sister – noisy, irritating and worst of all, not even a *real* movie fan. Rose only liked soppy films about animals and ballet dancers and animated fairies. When she didn't like a movie, she would ask dumb questions all the way through in a very loud voice.

'Doesn't matter what's fair, your mum's got a meeting at the health centre tonight and she can't leave Rose alone in the house.' Mum was a district nurse and had to attend meetings at the most inconvenient times.

'Perfect,' muttered Kip. He upended the large bag of corn kernels into the mouth of the machine and hit the start button. There was a brief pause and then a series of popping sounds. Huge knobbles of popcorn began to spill from the dispenser, filling the booth with their delicious aroma.

The glass door of the cinema swung open and Norman plodded in. Despite the warm summer evening, he was wearing a heavy overcoat and had a woollen scarf wrapped around his neck. He trudged over to the counter and stood watching Kip for a moment. Then he spoke in his familiar mournful tones.

'Making popcorn?' he asked.

Kip looked at him. He felt like saying, *No, I'm juggling with porridge,* but he didn't. Norman could be touchy at the best of times and, since he was only going to be around for a couple more days, it wouldn't do to upset him. So he smiled and nodded.

'Yeah,' he said. 'I thought I'd get it started. Crowd'll be coming in soon.'

'Think you'll *get* a crowd for this?' asked Norman gloomily.

'Sure. It's had great reviews.'

Norman leaned over the counter to speak in confidence. 'Any luck with my replacement?' he murmured. 'I have to be gone by Sunday. Kitty's driving over in the Punto to collect my bits and pieces.'

'Er...Dad got a letter just now,' said Kip, 'from a guy who used to work at Il Fanto...Il Fant...this cinema in Venice.'

'Venice?' Norman raised his bushy grey eyebrows at this. 'What kind of a cinema would that be? The city's all underwater, isn't it?'

'Maybe they give you a snorkel and flippers at the door,' suggested Kip and he started to laugh, but Norman just looked at him blankly.

'How would you be able to hear anything?' he asked.

Kip shook his head. Norman must have had his sense of humour surgically removed at a young age. 'Shouldn't you be er...getting things ready in the projection room?' he asked hopefully.

'All sorted,' said Norman. 'Spliced the reels together this afternoon. Adverts, trailers, feature, the lot. All set to go at the flick of a switch.'

'Oh.' Kip returned his attention to the popcorn machine, which had now filled the heated glass box to the halfway mark. 'How er...how's your lumbago?' he asked, trying to make conversation.

'Oh, dreadful, but I don't like to grumble.' This was a lie; Norman *loved* to grumble. 'It's what you get when you spend your life standing around in cold projection rooms.' He leaned further over the counter, as if to confide a secret. 'Now, about my leaving present,' he said.

Kip stared at him. He hadn't been aware that there was going to *be* one.

'I don't want your father spending too much on me. I know he's got money troubles at the moment. So, just something modest. And perhaps a nicely worded card?'

'Right,' said Kip. 'I'll ... mention it.'

'Good lad.'

The entrance door swung open again and Kip glanced up, expecting to see the first of the night's crowd arriving early, but the man who now stood in the foyer was not a regular and, frankly, Kip thought he was one of the oddest-looking people he had ever seen.

He was tall and whip-thin, dressed in a long, black leather coat that came almost to his ankles. He wore a black, wide-brimmed hat that cast a shadow onto his face, and from out of that shadow, peered two fierce eyes that were the palest shade of grey. There was hardly any flesh on the face at all. The cheeks were sunken, the skin unnaturally pale. Kip had the impression that he was looking at somebody very old and yet the man's tall figure seemed incredibly wiry and full of vitality. He lifted a hand and Kip saw that he was wearing tight, black leather gloves that seemed to cling to his long fingers like a second skin.

'The Paramount!' he said, in a strangely accented voice. *Italian*? 'Oh yes, there's quite a history here, I can *smell* it.' His gaze seemed to focus on Kip, and his mouth shaped itself into a grin, revealing two rows of perfectly-shaped tombstone-white teeth. 'You, boy,' he said. 'Where is the owner of this fine establishment?'

'He's er...he's in the office.'

'Then would you be kind enough to tell him that Mr Lazarus is here to see him?' The man turned to Norman. 'And you, of course, are the projectionist. I smell celluloid on you.'

Norman looked slightly offended.

'I had a bath this morning,' he said.

'It weaves itself into the pores,' said Mr Lazarus. 'Don't worry, it is a fine smell – the smell of adventure and drama and romance.' He studied Norman for a moment. 'So, you're finally giving up on it, are you?'

'I beg your pardon,' said Norman.

'Moving on. Deserting this fine theatre of dreams where you have worked for...' He paused for a moment as though considering, 'For fifty years,' he said, with conviction.

'Good Lord,' said Norman. 'That's exactly right.

But how did you—?'

'It is my business to know,' said Mr Lazarus, as if this explained everything. 'And only a fool would come ill-prepared to an interview.' He returned his attention to Kip. 'Your father?' he enquired.

'Er...yeah, just a minute.' Kip moved to the adjoining door, thinking as he did so that he hadn't actually mentioned that the owner *was* his father. He pushed open the door and stuck his head through. 'Dad,' he said, 'there's a Mr Lazarus here to see you.' And he raised his eyebrows as if to say, *Wait till you meet this guy!*

Dad got up from the desk and came through, looking a bit flustered.

'Mr Lazarus,' he said. 'I wish you'd let me know you were calling tonight, I'd have—'

'Put out the red carpet?' said Mr Lazarus, with the ghost of a smile.

'Er...' Dad extended a hand across the counter to shake but Mr Lazarus didn't oblige. Instead, he lifted a gloved hand. One moment the hand was empty, the next there was a small square of cardboard gripped between thumb and forefinger. 'My card,' he said and handed it to Dad with a melodramatic flourish. Dad examined it blankly for a moment and then passed it to Kip. Kip looked at it. It was just a square of white card with the word LAZARUS printed on it in black letters – but, as he stared at it, something amazing

11

happened, something that almost made him drop the card.

For an instant, it seemed to become a small screen and, on the screen, Kip saw, in incredible detail, an ancient primeval forest and, moving through that forest, an olive-green Tyrannosaurus Rex charging after some unseen prey, smashing down the vegetation with its huge back legs, its mighty jaws open to crush and tear its prey. Then, just as suddenly, the image shimmered and vanished and it was simply a square of card again. Kip swallowed and put it down on the counter, stunned. Dad didn't seem to have noticed anything odd. He looked perfectly calm.

'So,' he said, 'you mentioned something in your letter about working in Venice. May I ask why you left your last position?'

Mr Lazarus's eyes seemed to moisten for a moment.

'Floods,' he said. 'The awful affliction that will one day overwhelm that entire city. Forgive me, but it makes me emotional to think of that wonderful old cinema, swamped by the rising waters and nothing we could do to save it. The owner, the incomparable Señor Ravelli, was obliged to walk away after so many years of hard work. Ah, how we cried when the news was given to us. How we wept! Do you know Il Fantoccini, Mr McCall?'

'I'm afraid not,' said Dad. 'We usually holiday in

Morecambe.' He paused, as though expecting a laugh, but he didn't get one. 'Do you . . . perhaps have a reference from Señor Ravelli?'

Mr Lazarus smiled thinly as though he'd just been insulted.

'Forgive me, Mr McCall, but a man such as myself needs no references. I have eaten, drunk and slept cinema, ever since I was the age of the boy who stands beside you. Your son, I have no doubt of that. I can see the resemblance.'

'Er . . . yes, this is Kip.' Then Dad indicated Norman. 'And this—'

'Is Norman Cresswell,' finished Mr Lazarus. 'A man famed throughout the world for his cinematic skills.'

'Really?' said Norman, looking doubtful. 'Oh, I don't know about that.'

'Mr Cresswell, you are a legend! Many people still speak of that night in nineteen seventy-nine, when the film snapped and you had it back up and running in less than two minutes, without missing a single frame.'

Norman looked bewildered. If such a thing had happened to him, it was clear that he didn't remember it.

'Well, I . . . pride myself on being a professional,' he said.

'Of course you do! Such a shame that poor health prevents you from continuing in this noble tradition.'

'It's my lumbago,' said Norman, making it sound almost like an apology. 'As the saying goes, Mr Lazarus, the spirit is willing...'

'But the flesh is weak. I know, I know.' He reached out a hand and patted Norman on the shoulder. 'My heart goes out to you, sir.' He paused, turned back to the counter. 'So, let me see...' He seemed to concentrate for a moment, as if marshalling his strength. 'This fine cinema was opened in nineteen twenty-three with a showing of *The Warrior Queen*, a silent movie for which a live orchestra provided an accompaniment.'

Kip happened to be looking at the card lying in front of him, and for a fraction of a second it showed another image: the Paramount Picture Palace in grainy black and white. A press of eager people stood round the entrance, the men all wearing hats, the ladies bonnets and fur coats. Kip was about to say something but, once again, the image shimmered and returned to blank white card.

Mr Lazarus continued speaking. 'The cinema has kept going ever since... your great-grandfather, your grandfather, your father and now you, Mr McCall, have worked tirelessly to achieve this... but, in nineteen ninety-six, a huge multiplex was opened only a short car journey from here, offering its customers the luxury of twelve screens and free parking. This had a huge impact on your fortunes.

14

Now, you struggle on in the knowledge that the coming digital revolution will probably finish you off completely.'

There was a long silence after that.

Eventually, Dad managed to find a few words. 'You've certainly done your homework,' he said.

Mr Lazarus smiled.

'Mr McCall, that's not homework. That's knowledge built up over a lifetime of devotion to the silver screen.'

'And may I ask what brought you to this area?' asked Dad.

'Isn't it obvious? There was a cinema that needed a projectionist. How could I stay away?'

'But... I only put the ad in the *Manchester Evening News* five days ago,' said Dad. 'If you came all the way from Venice, then—'

'I got here as quickly as I could,' said Mr Lazarus. 'The show must go on, Mr McCall. That is my motto.'

'Well, er... that's marvellous. I'm sure Norman here will be happy to take you up to the projection room to er... show you how everything works.'

'No need,' Mr Lazarus assured him. He lifted his hands as if framing a scene. 'The projection room is long and narrow. You have just the one projector, a nineteen fifties Westar system, a fine piece of machinery still running smoothly after all these years.'

15

'That's absolutely right,' gasped Norman.

'To the left there is a tower of spools where the spliced film runs to the projector. Because of the narrowness of the room, the film has to be twisted by forty-five degrees in order to run through the shutter. Unusual, but it works. You use an ordinary anamorphic lens to show the adverts and then switch to cinemascope for the trailers and main feature.'

Now Norman was staring at him, his mouth open. 'How could you possibly know all that?' he gasped.

'Experience,' said Mr Lazarus. 'So, Mr Cresswell, your last night here is . . . ?'

'Tomorrow,' said Norman. 'You see, on Sunday—'

'Kitty is driving over in the Punto,' finished Mr Lazarus. 'How is your sister, Mr Cresswell?'

'You know Kitty?'

'I know *of* her. And I'm sure she is going to make your retirement very comfortable.' Mr Lazarus considered for a moment. 'In that case, I shall be here tomorrow at seven-thirty prompt for the handover. If it is all right with you, I shall run the last show while you observe that everything is done to your satisfaction. I think after so long in this business, you deserve to take it easy on your final night.'

'Well . . . that would be a novelty,' admitted Norman.

'Excellent.' The entrance doors opened and the first of the evening's audience started to wander into the foyer. Mr Lazarus made a formal bow. 'Well, I see your audience is arriving, so I shall leave you to your work. Till tomorrow!'

And with that, he turned and strode towards the door. Dad, Kip and Norman watched him go. It seemed that the interview was over and the Paramount had a new projectionist – yet to Kip it felt rather like he and Dad had been the ones who'd just been interviewed. But customers were approaching the ticket office and there was no time to discuss the matter further. Dad scooted through to the ticket office while Norman made his way into the auditorium, looking slightly dazed.

And Kip…Kip just stood there looking at the white card lying on the counter, willing it to show one of those amazing images again. But nothing happened. Not that night, anyway.

CHAPTER THREE

THE SHOW MUST GO ON

There was a good-sized audience that night. By ten to eight, the foyer was filling up with eager customers and Kip was obliged to crack open another big bag of corn kernels. He was kept busy, shovelling hot popcorn into containers and dishing out Cokes, Maltesers and other goodies. Over in the office, Dad was looking a bit happier than he had before, as hard cash began to change hands. If this was how it was on Friday, then Saturday and Sunday promised to do big business.

At five to eight, Beth came in for her weekly fix of movies and popcorn. You could set your watch by her. She was twelve years old and in Kip's class at school. She was thin and tomboyish, with large chocolate-brown eyes, her black hair cut in a short bob. She knew more about movies than any other girl Kip had met. She took her place in the queue for popcorn and smiled at Kip when she got to the counter.

'Hi, Kip,' she said. 'Busy tonight.'

Kip shovelled popcorn into a medium-sized ...king what she wanted. She always had the same thing. Then he reached into the fridge for a Diet Coke. 'Bad news,' he told her, 'Rose will be joining us.'

Beth smiled.

'I don't mind answering the odd question,' she said.

'The odd *very odd* question,' Kip corrected her, taking her money. 'What did she ask me last time? Oh yeah, "Isn't that actor in Coronation Street?"'

'What's so odd about that?'

'She was talking about Johnny Depp!'

Beth laughed. Kip liked it when she did that, it did something weird to her face, making her look almost pretty.

There was an uncomfortable silence – then Beth's gaze fell on Mr Lazarus's card, which still lay on the counter top. 'What's this?' she asked, reaching for it. But before she could get there, Kip snatched it away from her.

'It's nothing,' he said, grabbing the card and pushing it into the back pocket of his jeans. He wasn't entirely sure why he'd done that. Perhaps he didn't want Beth seeing something odd and asking awkward questions. He wanted to examine the card himself first, to see if he could figure out how it worked. He gave Beth her change.

'Save me a seat,' he said, and she headed in the direction of the auditorium. 'And one for Rose!' he shouted after her.

He went back to serving popcorn and dishing out sweets. He kept glancing up at the clock on the foyer wall. The film started at ten past eight and the trick was to make sure everybody was served by then. Dad could always cover for the odd straggler arriving after show time. But where was Rose? Woe betide him if he went in without her.

As if in answer to his thought, the door opened and his sister stepped through. Kip caught a brief glimpse of his mother, waving a hand at him, before vanishing in to the night. Mum didn't much care for the Paramount, especially since it had fallen on hard times. Dad told Kip once that when he and Mum were first married, she had loved the place and thought it a great adventure to be co-owner of her own cinema. But over the years, as she had watched Dad struggling to keep the place going, the novelty had worn off, and these days she regarded the Paramount as a great big weight around both their necks. There was a time when Mum had come out to watch the odd movie here, but not anymore.

Rose marched over, looking the picture of innocence and stepped straight to the front of the queue.

'I want popcorn,' she said.

Kip looked apologetically at the people she had just bypassed.

'Rose,' he said. 'There's a queue.'

She turned and looked at it, almost absent-mindedly, as though checking that he wasn't lying. Then she turned back.

'And some Skittles,' she said. 'Mummy said I could.'

Kip ground his teeth and told himself not to get annoyed in front of the customers. It looked bad. He filled a huge box with popcorn and handed it down. It looked almost as big as her. She stood there, looking up at him expectantly, both hands holding the box.

'Skittles,' she reminded him.

'Yes, yes.' He got them from the display and held them out to her, but she didn't have a spare hand to take them.

'I'll bring them in for you,' he promised her.

'You're not to eat any,' she warned him.

'I won't. I don't like Skittles.'

'I'll know if you eat one,' she said.

'Will you go inside, please?' he asked her. 'I've got people to serve. Beth is saving a seat for you.'

She nodded, almost wearily, and turned to go. Kip looked at the next customer with a forced grin. 'Sorry about that,' he said. 'She's my sister.'

'She's cute,' said the lady at the head of the queue.

Yeah, thought Kip, *cute as a rattlesnake*. He knew it was wrong to think like that. He knew that he was supposed to care about Rose and look after her and all that, but sometimes she could be really hard work. He went back to scooping popcorn.

By two minutes past eight, there were only a few stragglers left to serve so Kip told Dad that he was heading into the auditorium.

'I want to watch the new trailers,' he explained. 'Can you manage?'

'I generally do,' muttered Dad, who had become well used to this Friday routine. 'You'd better hurry up. You don't want to keep your girlfriend waiting.'

'You're hilarious,' Kip told him. 'You should be on TV.'

He grabbed a bag of Skittles for Rose, went out through the office and hurried into the darkened cinema.

CHAPTER FOUR

COMING ATTRACTIONS

He'd timed it perfectly, arriving just as the trailer for next week's movie, *Terror Island*, came on. It looked great. As Kip came down the aisle between the seats, some frightened-looking people were running through a dark forest, being pursued by a ravenous sabre-toothed tiger. Kip went to the front row on the right-hand side and slipped into the empty seat that Beth had saved for him.

'Where's my sweets?' he heard Rose demand, so he passed the Skittles to Beth, who passed them to Rose.

Now on screen, a terrified-looking woman was pushing open a door, beyond which lay total darkness.

Don't go in there, thought Kip. But she did. They *always* did in films like this. She took a step into the dark room and then she heard a noise – a sort of squelching sound. 'Hello?' she called. 'Is that you, Tad?' Kip shook his head. Whoever, or whatever, it was, you could be pretty sure it wasn't somebody or something you wanted to bump into down a dark alley. 'Hello?' she called again. Suddenly, something absolutely horrible lurched out of the darkness with a sound like water going down a plughole and Kip nearly jumped out of his seat.

Now the image cut to a group of people running down corridors. They were being pursued by several shambling figures; ugly slope-headed creatures dressed in furs and armed with lethal wooden clubs. They were gibbering like apes and baring their yellow teeth.

'What are they?' whispered Kip.

'Neanderthals,' said Beth knowingly.

'What's Number Tails?' asked Rose.

'Cavemen,' said Beth.

She held out a box of popcorn to Kip and he took a handful without taking his eyes off the screen.

'Looks great,' he whispered.

'It looks *'orrible*!' said Rose's voice and Kip had to smile.

He and Beth always chose to sit here in the front row, with the screen towering over them. It helped make it feel like they were actually *in* the film. This, in fact, was Kip's biggest ambition – to be in a movie. Oh, he knew he'd never be an actor or anything like that, but maybe one day he could be a bit player in something like this. He'd love to dress up as a monster and go running round in the dark, making the actresses scream. He didn't suppose it would ever happen, but it was nice to have a dream.

There was a final image of a sabre-toothed tiger leaping straight at the screen, its jaws open as if to swallow the camera. Then the title came up in blood-red letters – *Terror Island*. The house lights came on briefly before the main feature and some twangy, old-fashioned guitar music began to play. Norman always put on exactly the same CD; something called *Mr Guitar Man Plays the Hits*.

'That film looks nasty,' said Rose. 'I'm not coming to see it.'

'Good,' said Kip. 'That suits me.' He settled back in his seat and then noticed that Beth was smiling at him. 'What's up with you?' he said.

'Must be nice having a sister.'

'Don't get me started,' said Kip, lowering his voice to a whisper so Rose wouldn't hear. 'It's OK for you, you're an only child.'

'Yes, but I wouldn't mind a little brother or sister to look after.'

'Look after? Wait on hand and foot, you mean! It never stops.'

Beth looked wistful.

'You don't know what you've got till it's gone,' she said.

'What's that supposed to mean?'

'It's something my mum says.'

Just then the lights started to go down. Kip sat there, savouring the moment of anticipation he always felt at such times. Up came the card with the film's title and the certificate on it. A brief pause.

Then came the opening credits. Ominous music began to build and the names of the actors appeared one by one. All of it was increasing Kip's anticipation of that first scene, the first thing the camera zoomed in on and . . .

There it was! A city scene and you knew instantly that this wasn't modern day because the cars were all black and clattery and the people strolling along the sidewalks wore old-fashioned clothes, and every single one of them was wearing a hat. Now the camera was homing in on the entrance to the FIRST NATIONAL BANK and . . .

The camera cut to a close-up of a car drawing to a halt outside the bank. The rear door opened and out stepped Russell Raven, dressed in a sharp pinstripe suit, a hat pulled down over his eyes. He had a long package under his arm wrapped in brown paper. The camera cut to other cars drawing up, more tough guys getting out, each of them carrying a similar package and looking mean.

The men began to stride in through the entrance of the bank, moving past a guard near the door, who looked ancient, and you just knew wasn't going to be any use at all if anything kicked off. The men walked to different places around the crowded bank and the camera cut to a clock on the wall; you could see that it was just two minutes to ten. A series of cuts showed each of the bad guys glancing at the clock and looking away and you knew they were waiting; they were waiting for ten o'clock.

Then there was an extreme close-up of the clock and in slow motion the minute hand clicked the last notch, with a sound like a mallet striking a lump of stone and then...then the mayhem began.

Russell Raven tore open the package, revealing a vicious-looking Tommy gun, he swung it at the people standing near him and yelled, 'Everybody on the floor! This is a stick-up!'

CHAPTER FIVE

BYE BYE, NORMAN

The scene was replaying itself in Kip's head as he stepped through the cinema entrance the following evening. It had been brilliant: fast, punchy and close enough to make you feel as though you were part of the action.

He found Dad sitting at his desk in the ticket office, looking a bit more positive than he had the night before. It had been one of the best Fridays in ages. As Kip came in Dad glanced slyly round and handed Kip a small gift box.

'What do you think?' he asked.

Kip opened it and found that it contained a cheap-looking digital watch.

'It's very nice and everything,' said Kip, 'but I've already got one.'

'It's not for you, you idiot! It's for Norman. It's his last night, I had to give him something after all these years, didn't I?'

Kip nodded. He tried to imagine the watch on Norman's wrist and somehow couldn't quite see it.

'You don't think it's a bit...trendy for him?' murmured Kip.

'I'm sure it is, but I was in a fix. I had half an hour to run into Manchester and a budget of twenty quid. I had to grab something fast.' He looked at Kip defensively. 'I got him a lovely card,' he added. 'And I've laid on a few bottles of wine and some dinky pies for afterwards.'

Kip shrugged and handed the box back to his dad.

'I'm sure it's better than a poke in the eye,' he said. 'Oh, by the way, Beth said she'd drop by after the film, to say goodbye and all that.'

'Oh yes?' Dad waggled his eyebrows. 'Getting serious, is it?'

'Don't be stupid. She just wants to say goodbye, that's all. Better keep that present hidden, Norman will be in soon.'

'He's already here. Went straight up to the projection room with a duster and some polish. Said he wanted it all to be spick-and-span for when Mr Lazarus arrived.' Dad frowned. 'What did you make of him, by the way? Didn't you think there was something . . . odd about him?'

'Odd? He was a complete weirdo.' Kip reached into the back pocket of his jeans and pulled out the business card. He'd spent a lot of time looking at it since last night, but not once had he seen anything else unexpected. 'Did you have a proper look at this thing?' he asked.

Dad grinned. 'Yeah. Great business card that, isn't

it? No address, no phone number, just a name. What use is it?'

'That's not what I mean. Did you ... did you see anything else when you looked at it?'

Dad seemed puzzled.

'Like what?' he asked.

'Oh, like a Tyran ... a big Tyran ...' Kip's voice trailed away. How could he explain what he'd seen without coming over as a complete nutter? 'Like an email address?' he finished lamely.

'No,' said Dad. 'Like I said, useless. But what about all that stuff he *knew*? He described our projection room as though he'd lived in the place. And he knew more about Norman than I do and I've worked with him for years!' Dad's expression darkened. 'Most baffling of all, if he really *was* living in Venice and I only put the advert in the *Manchester Evening News* six days ago, how in the name of God did he manage to get himself over here in time to—'

'I flew,' said a voice from the open doorway and Kip and Dad nearly jumped out of their skins. Mr Lazarus was leaning against the doorframe, his arms crossed, an amused smile on his thin lips. 'You've no idea how tired my arms were.'

'Oh ... er ... sorry, we didn't hear you come in,' stuttered Dad. 'I hope that didn't sound rude.'

'It did, now you mention it, but there's no problem.' Mr Lazarus sauntered into the office and stood beside the desk. He noticed the gift box lying there and reached out a gloved hand to tap it with his forefinger. 'It looks as though somebody is going to receive a little gift tonight,' he said.

'Oh, yes, just something for Norman, to mark his retirement,' said Dad. 'It's really not very much.'

'Everybody appreciates a gift,' said Mr Lazarus. 'And a watch is always a nice present, don't you think?'

Kip and Dad exchanged glances. The box was closed.

'How do you *do* that?' asked Kip.

Mr Lazarus gave him a look of pure innocence.

'A simple deduction,' he said. 'What else would you give somebody after so many years of faithful service? A watch is the traditional gift, no?' He smiled. 'Oh, Mr McCall, I just wanted to warn you, I'll be having some equipment delivered tomorrow morning. I'll get the keys from Norman tonight and I will be there to organise carrying the boxes up to the projection room.'

'What kind of equipment?' asked Dad warily.

'Just my own little bits and pieces,' said Mr Lazarus. 'Over the years I have developed my own particular way of doing things. I can assure you it won't interfere with the normal running of the cinema; in fact, I think you will be delighted with the results. Oh yes, before I forget.' He lifted a hand with a flourish and a large brown envelope appeared magically in his fingers. 'You might want to look at these,' he said, handing the envelope to Dad.

'What are they?' asked Mr McCall.

'You wanted references, did you not? I found a few scraps of information among my papers that I thought might interest you.'

'I'll er...look at them when I've got a spare moment,' said Dad. 'Thanks for bringing them in. Anyway...' He glanced at his watch. 'Kip, it's half seven, we'd better get the popcorn on.'

Mr Lazarus smiled. 'And I'd better get up to the projection room. Poor Norman has been working so hard up there, cleaning and polishing. There was really no need for him to go to such trouble. I'll see you after the film. For the party.'

He seemed to glide out of the ticket office and around to the doors of the auditorium. Dad shook his head.

'Did you tell him about the party?' he asked.

'No. Maybe Norman did.'

'Norman doesn't know,' said Dad. 'That's why they call it a *surprise* party.'

'Oh yeah,' said Kip. He shrugged his shoulders. 'Maybe Mr Lazarus is a mind-reader.'

He went through into the sweet kiosk and switched on the popcorn machine, telling himself as he did so that, the first chance he got he was going to have a look at Mr Lazarus's references, to see if they might give him any clues about the mysterious projectionist.

It was a Saturday night, usually the best night of the week, and sure enough the place was almost three quarters full, so Dad was very pleased. After the crowd had drifted out, Kip helped to set up the refreshments on a table in the foyer, while Dad fetched the bottles of wine he had stored in the office and some paper cups left over from Christmas. Beth called in with a card she'd bought for Norman. Minnie, the lady who helped clean the cinema over the weekend, turned up too, and Dad had invited several regular customers to join them.

'Help yourselves to drinks from the fridge,' Dad told Beth and Kip. He set the box of wine on the table, opened the flaps and lifted out a bottle. He stared at it for a moment.

'That's odd,' he said.

'What?' asked Kip.

Dad was taking out other bottles. 'These aren't the wines I bought.'

Kip stared at him. 'They must be,' he said.

Dad shook his head. 'No way. I bought supermarket plonk at four quid a go. This stuff...' He peered at the label of the bottle he was holding. '*Sangiovese*,' he read. '*Chianti Classico. 1945...*'

His jaw dropped. 'Good grief, Kip, this is vintage wine. It must have cost a flipping bomb!' He peered into the box as though expecting to see other cheaper bottles in there. Instead, he pulled out something wrapped in tissue paper. He unwrapped it to discover a crystal wine glass. 'There's more of them in here,' he said. 'There's even a corkscrew. I don't understand. It's the same box but...'

At that moment, the door of the auditorium opened and Norman and Mr Lazarus strolled out, deep in conversation – or, at least, Mr Lazarus was talking while Norman listened intently. He glanced up at the small gathering in surprise.

'Oh, hello,' he said. 'What's all this, then?'

'Just a little farewell party,' Dad told him. 'To say thank you for all your hard work over the years. Will you have white or red, Norman?'

'Oh, well,' said Norman. 'I don't normally drink alcohol but, as it's a special occasion, I'll have a little drop of red.' Dad uncorked a bottle and filled a couple of the crystal glasses. 'Mr Lazarus?'

'I'll go for the *Tocai Fruliano*,' he said. 'Fifty-one *was* a spectacular year.'

Dad looked at him.

'So this must be your doing,' he said.

'I hope you don't mind,' said Mr Lazarus. 'I thought an occasion like this demanded something special – and, of course, you cannot drink vintage wine from a paper cup.' Dad filled a glass with white wine and handed it to him, then passed out drinks to the other guests.

'You must let me know what you've spent,' he told Mr Lazarus. 'I can't allow you to pay for this out of the pittance I'm going to be paying you . . .' Dad looked mortified. 'Oh, my goodness,' he said. 'We never even discussed your salary, did we?'

Mr Lazarus waved a hand in dismissal.

'It is no great matter, Mr McCall. Pay me whatever you used to pay Norman. And as for the wine . . . well, that is my pleasure. Consider it my little contribution to this charming party.'

'You're really too generous.' Dad picked up his glass of red and then lifted it in a toast. 'Well, we all know why we're here tonight, to say thank you to Norman, who has been a vital part of the Paramount for so many years. We really couldn't have kept going without him. To Norman,' he said, 'wishing you every happiness in your retirement.'

'To Norman!' everyone raised their glasses in unison and they all drank.

Norman looked around, a little misty-eyed.

'How kind,' he said. 'I wasn't expecting anything like this.'

Kip stepped forward with the cards and handed them to Norman. There was an awkward silence while he opened each of them and examined them in great detail. Beth had actually found a card featuring an old black-and-white photograph of a silent-movie cinematographer. The message inside read, *To The World's Greatest Movie Buff.*

'It took me ages to find the right card,' said Beth. 'No idea who the guy in the picture is, but I thought you'd like it.'

Mr Lazarus leaned across to look at the photograph.

'It's Wallace Evans,' he said. 'A charming fellow, very fond of chocolate cake, as I remember.'

'You . . . know him?' gasped Beth.

'I *knew* him,' said Mr Lazarus. 'He's gone now, of course. But we had some happy times together.'

Now Dad stepped forward with the gift box.

'We've bought you something,' he said. 'It's really not very much and, of course, if the style doesn't suit, you can always exchange it for something else.'

'I'm sure it will be perfect,' said Norman. 'Thank you so much.' He opened the box and looked at the contents. For a few moments he said nothing and Kip couldn't really blame him. The trendy watch wasn't a suitable present for a man of his age, he probably wouldn't be seen dead in something like that. Then Norman let out a gasp and his eyes filled up. 'It's beautiful,' he murmured. 'Exquisite.'

Kip and Dad exchanged glances. Kip thought he

was laying it on a bit thick for a twenty-quid digital with a plastic strap.

'It's nothing really,' protested Dad. 'There wasn't a lot of time and—' He broke off in baffled silence, because now Norman was taking the watch from the box – but it wasn't the watch that had been in there before. It was a large silver pocket watch on a length of chain. Norman turned it over in his hand and he gasped again. 'You've had it engraved!' he cried.

'Have we?' asked Dad incredulously.

Dad and Kip could only stand and stare as Norman read out what was inscribed on the watch's silver case. '*To Norman with much affection from all your friends at the Paramount.*' He looked up at Dad. 'This is too much!' he protested.

Dad looked like he was in total agreement.

'I . . . I don't quite understand . . .' he mumbled. 'I only . . .'

'Open the watch,' suggested Mr Lazarus, pointing. 'You see, there's a little catch there.'

Norman pressed the catch and the silver cover flipped open. The watch began to play a familiar tinkling tune.

'The theme from *The Godfather*!' said Norman. 'My all-time favourite film!' He stared at Dad. 'How did you know?'

'Er . . . because er . . . you . . . you must have . . .

mentioned it some time?' Dad lifted his glass of wine and took a large gulp of the contents.

Kip's mind was racing. How was such a thing possible? He could understand how Mr Lazarus might have substituted the wine, but he had only been told about the gift two hours earlier, before the showing had started. The box had been on Dad's desk ever since and, as far as Kip was aware, Mr Lazarus had been up in the projection room, all through the film. And besides, even if he had sneaked away for a few moments, there was nowhere around here where you could buy a watch like that and get it engraved in a couple of hours.

'Well, thank you all so much,' said Norman. 'I'll treasure this.' He returned the watch to its box and slipped it into his pocket. Then he took a large gulp of his wine. 'You know, this is the nicest wine I've ever tasted,' he said. 'I do believe I'll have another glass!'

Dad dutifully topped him up.

'It is lovely,' he agreed. 'We have Mr Lazarus to thank for that.' He studied the tall thin man for a moment, as though trying to figure him out. 'While we're making toasts, I suppose we really should have another one,' he said. 'To the man who's going to take over from our Norman. A man who has already made some…amazing changes. To Mr Lazarus!'

'Mr Lazarus!' everyone said and they all drank to his health. He stood there, looking back at them, his grey eyes regarding them, a half-smile on his thin lips; and Kip found himself wondering what other changes he might have in store for the Paramount.

CHAPTER SIX

NEW EQUIPMENT

Kip woke early the next morning and couldn't get back to sleep. A weird mixture of thoughts and questions kept bubbling through his head and they all had to do with Mr Lazarus. How did that 'business card' of his work? How had he managed to switch Norman's wine and present without anybody noticing? And how did he know so much about a cinema he had never visited before?

Eventually, Kip got up and slouched downstairs in his pyjamas. He found a note from Mum on the kitchen table, saying that she'd had to drive over to work to help out with an 'unexpected crisis'. He was to let Dad sleep late, because Mum thought he was looking very tired. Kip sighed. He popped a couple of slices of bread into the toaster and switched on the kettle.

When he'd finished breakfast, Kip put his plate in the dishwasher and went through to Dad's study. He switched on the computer and, while he was waiting for it to boot up, he noticed a brown envelope lying on the desk. It was the envelope that Mr Lazarus had given Dad the day before.

He looked inside and saw a sheath of papers of various sizes. They were old and mottled, clearly not photocopies but originals. He set them down on the desk and started to leaf through them. They were mostly articles cut from newspapers, though annoyingly there was nothing on any of them to identify when they had been published. However, they all looked ancient, the typefaces all higgledy-piggledy, everything set out in little columns and boxes. When he looked closer, he realised that they weren't even in English, but what looked like Italian; he wondered how Mr Lazarus had expected Dad to be able to decipher them.

Kip turned the pages, hoping to find something that he could actually read but then his eye was caught by a black-and-white photograph of a cinema. Carved into its stonework was the name *Il Fantoccini*. And on the hording in front of the cinema was what must have been the title of the film they were showing, *Cabiria*. Several people were posed proudly on the steps at the entrance.

Closest to the camera stood a man in a top hat, tail coat and those weird black shoes with white toecaps on them. He wore white gloves and was leaning on a walking stick. He had a thick, black moustache that made him look like a walrus and he was smiling at the camera and lifting his free hand in a gesture that seemed to say, *Behold, my cinema!* This, Kip decided, must have been the Señor Ravelli that Mr Lazarus had mentioned. Other people stood a polite distance behind him: several men wearing military-style uniforms with flat-peaked caps and epaulettes on their shoulders, and a younger man, dressed in a fancy waistcoat and striped trousers. He was gazing proudly at the camera, hands on hips, a half-smile on his face. Kip gasped because there was no mistaking who it was. He was looking at a much younger version of Mr Lazarus.

Kip leafed through the rest of the papers but found nothing else he was able to read. So he got Google up on the computer and typed Il Fantoccini into the search box. Up came a series of articles but none of them seemed to have anything to do with a cinema of that name.

He decided to try another tack and typed in *Cabiria*. The first hit revealed that it was a silent movie, directed by somebody called Giovanni Pastrone, released in . . .' Kip stared at the screen and had to check another couple of sites to make sure there had been no mistake. They all agreed on the release date. 1914. Kip found the photograph and looked at it again. Though the cinema was undoubtedly old-fashioned, in the picture it looked brand spanking new, freshly painted and clean as a whistle. He looked again at the young man in the waistcoat. It *was* Mr Lazarus, he was sure of that, not his father or his grandfather. But if this really was the cinema's opening day and the film it was showing was fresh on release, then that made Mr Lazarus . . . Kip counted in his head, not really wanting to believe.

Assuming he was in his teens in the photograph, that would make him way over a hundred years old. While Kip could accept that he was pretty elderly and might actually be some years older than he looked, this was pushing it a bit.

He remembered Mr Lazarus saying something about equipment that was being delivered to the cinema this morning, so he logged off the computer and went back upstairs to get dressed, dragging on a T-shirt and a pair of jeans. He glanced into Dad's room but he was still snoring soundly, the covers pulled up around his head. He checked Rose's room and she too was out for the count, her eyes closed, her golden hair fanned out on the pillow around her. She looked cute when she was like this, but Kip wasn't fooled for a moment. Any minute now she'd be up, demanding that he play with her and her collection of Barbie dolls.

He went downstairs again, grabbed his jacket and keys and walked quickly to the Paramount, just in time to see a large van driving away.

The foyer was deserted, so Kip made his way up to the projection room. The door was open and there were noises from within, the gentle clinking of metal against metal. Kip could see that Mr Lazarus was busy setting up an elaborate piece of equipment alongside the projector. He had taken his leather coat off and was wearing a richly-embroidered waistcoat, very like the one he had been wearing in the old photograph. The equipment was like nothing that Kip had ever seen before and seemed to consist of a round wooden platform set on a couple of metal rails. As Kip watched, Mr Lazarus slid the platform backwards and forward, occasionally squirting a drop of oil from an old-fashioned canister onto the tracks. He never turned his head to look, but when he spoke it was evident that he knew who he was talking to.

'Well, don't just stand there, boy, come along inside.'

Kip stepped sheepishly into the room.

'Er...hi,' he said. 'I remembered you were having stuff delivered and I thought you...you might like some help.'

'That's very kind of you.' Mr Lazarus turned his head for a moment and studied Kip. Kip had the unpleasant sensation that he was being scrutinised by somebody who knew everything that went on inside his head. Mr Lazarus waved a hand at an open toolbox. 'Grab yourself a screwdriver,' he said. 'You can help me tighten this track.'

Kip picked up a screwdriver.

'Er...what do you want me to—?'

'Just tighten all the fittings,' Mr Lazarus told him. 'There mustn't be the slightest movement in any of it.'

Kip did as he was told and found that the strangely-shaped screwdriver fitted perfectly into the strangely-shaped screw heads.

'What *is* this thing?' he asked, mystified.

Mr Lazarus paused long enough to look at him. 'This,' he said, with a flourish of a gloved hand, 'is the Lazarus Enigma.' And with that he went back to work.

'I see,' said Kip. 'That's...great.' He thought for a moment. 'And what exactly does the Lazarus Enema—'

'Enigma!'

'Yes. What exactly does it do?'

Mr Lazarus sighed. 'It is my own invention. It does many things but one of its main purposes is to...enhance film.'

'Enhance it, *how*?'

'Films shown using this apparatus look sharper, clearer, more lifelike. It improves sound quality too.'

'Wow. Like digital?' asked Kip, but Mr Lazarus made a face as though somebody had just shoved an unpleasant-tasting sweet into his mouth.

'Don't mention that word,' he growled. 'That's nothing to do with cinema.'

'But everybody says it's the future,' said Kip.

'Pah! I speak of *real* cinema. The miracle that happens when millions of still images are fed through a shutter at twenty-four frames a second. Digital is an abomination. I will have nothing to do with it!'

'But Dad says—'

'You know,' said Mr Lazarus, 'we will get more done if we talk less.'

Kip took the hint and went on with his screw tightening. As he did so, he took the opportunity to glance around the cramped confines of the room and he noticed, amongst all the boxes and cases, an ancient folding bed propped up against one wall.

'What's the bed for?' he asked.

Mr Lazarus sighed and paused in his work.

'When somebody gets to my age, occasionally it is nice to have a little lie down,' he said.

Kip studied him for a moment.

'I wanted to ask you about that,' he said, 'about your age, I mean.'

Now Mr Lazarus turned and looked at Kip, a sardonic smile on his face.

'Don't you know it's rude to ask a question like that?' he said.

Kip felt his face reddening.

'It's just that I looked at those papers you gave to Dad—'

46

'Did you, now? I was under the impression that they were for his eyes only.'

'Er...well...I saw the photograph of Il Fanto... Il Fan...that cinema you used to work at. And it really looked like you in the picture.'

Mr Lazarus nodded but didn't say anything.

'And the film that was showing. Carri-whatsit? According to Wikipedia, that was released in 1914.'

Mr Lazarus was still looking at him. He seemed faintly amused by Kip's discomfort.

'What of it?' he asked.

'Well, let's say you were eighteen in that picture that would make you...well, more than a hundred years old, wouldn't it?'

Mr Lazarus considered for a moment.

'I suppose it would,' he said. 'Assuming, of course, it was a *first* showing of the film. But it could be that we were running a revival. It could be that the picture was taken in 1924...or 1946...or 1951.'

He went back to his tinkering. Kip waited for quite a while before he asked, 'Well, which one was it?'

Mr Lazarus shrugged his shoulders. 'I forget,' he said. 'My memory is not what it used to be.' He looked at Kip again. 'Any other questions bothering you?'

'Yes,' said Kip. He reached into his back pocket and pulled out the card. 'How does this work?'

Mr Lazarus looked at it.

'It's a business card,' he said. 'You give them to people.'

'Oh, yeah? With no address or phone number? What use is that? And besides, when I looked at it the first time...'

'Yes?'

'I saw something. On the card. I saw...'

Mr Lazarus leaned a little closer. He looked intrigued.

'What did you see, Kip? Describe it to me.'

Kip frowned.

'It was...well, I saw this, like, T. Rex? And it was running through a forest, smashing all the trees down.'

Mr Lazarus nodded. He seemed impressed.

'I think people see what they want to see,' he said. 'You like films with prehistoric monsters in them, yes?'

Kip nodded. 'I suppose,' he said.

'Well then.'

'Yeah, but I've looked at it lots since then and I haven't seen anything.'

'It doesn't happen every time. You have to be in the right frame of mind. Stop expecting to see something and that's when it might work.' Mr Lazarus went over to a cardboard box. He kneeled down and opened it, then took out an oddly-shaped lump of transparent glass.

'What's that?' asked Kip.

'It's a prism,' said Mr Lazarus. He stood and carried it back to the Lazarus Enigma, then began to attach it to an upright metal pole that stuck up from the side of the round platform.

'And what does that do?' asked Kip.

Mr Lazarus looked at him.

'Kip, you seem like a nice enough boy,' he said. 'But I have to say, you ask far too many questions.'

'Sorry,' said Kip. 'I'm just interested, that's all.'

Mr Lazarus switched on the projector. Then he slid the platform smoothly forward along the rails. Kip saw that there was something else new. A small mirror had been attached to the side of the projector. This reflected the beam of light into the prism, which, in turn, projected another beam down onto the round platform. Mr Lazarus looked pleased.

'Now,' he said. 'Everything is ready.'

'For what?' asked Kip, baffled.

'The Lazarus Enigma is activated.'

'Oh yeah? That's great.' Kip frowned. 'But . . .'

'Yes?' asked Mr Lazarus.

'You haven't told me what it does. I mean, you said it enhances film. But you also said it does many things. What are some of the other things it does?'

Mr Lazarus sighed. He studied Kip thoughtfully for a moment.

'Supposing I just show you?' he asked. 'How would that suit you?'

Kip shrugged.

'That would be OK, I guess,' he said.

'Very well. I was going to wait for a better time, but you're here and you're clearly interested, so...' Mr Lazarus clapped his gloved hands together. He got to his feet and walked over to the projector. 'Come over here,' he said.

Kip got to his feet and did as he was told. The old man indicated the wooden platform.

'Stand there,' he said.

Kip lifted his feet to climb onto the platform.

'Like this?' he asked.

'Perfect.'

'Well, what now?'

'Just a moment. There are a few things we have to do first.' Mr Lazarus reached into the pocket of his waistcoat and pulled out an odd-looking oval object hung on a length of chain. It seemed to be made of Perspex and had a round metal cover on the front of it. Kip could see that something beneath the cover was pulsing slowly on and off with a dull red glow that illuminated the Perspex. Mr Lazarus reached out and hung the object around Kip's neck.

'What's this for?' asked Kip curiously, lifting it in his fingers to get a better look.

'Don't touch that,' snapped Mr Lazarus. 'That's not a toy, Kip; it's the Lazarus Retriever.'

'Oh, right,' said Kip. He let the thing drop to the end of its chain. 'What's that then?'

'Never mind,' said Mr Lazarus. 'You might want to slip it beneath your T-shirt. You don't want to lose that.'

'No,' agreed Kip, bewildered, but he did as he was told.

'Now,' said Mr Lazarus, 'there's just one other thing...' He had turned away and was rooting amongst a jumble of rubbish on a worktop. After a few moments, he turned back, carrying what looked like a leather holster. 'Strap this around your waist,' he told Kip, handing it to him.

Kip buckled it around his skinny hips feeling rather like a cowboy donning a set of pistols, but this holster held only a brick-shaped gadget made of what looked like black Bakelite. It was studded with knobs and dials and switches.

'And this?' asked Kip, securing the buckle.

'The Lazarus Communicator,' said Mr Lazarus, wearily. 'Goodness, you ask a lot of questions!'

'I'm sorry,' muttered Kip. 'I was only wondering.'

'You'll find out soon enough,' said Mr Lazarus. 'I'll contact you when you're there and explain *everything*.'

Kip scratched his head.

'When I'm *where*?' he asked.

'In the film,' said Mr Lazarus. 'Now. Are you ready?'

But Kip was staring at him, completely baffled.

'In the film?' he echoed. 'I don't get it.'

'You will,' Mr Lazarus assured him. With one hand, he set the projector running; and with the other, he placed a hand against Kip's back and pushed him hard. The platform slid forward on its oiled wheels, straight into the light. Kip experienced a sudden wave of panic, rising within him.

'Wait a minute,' he said. 'I'm not sure I—'

But then a bright light was blazing into his face and almost instantly he felt a weird change coming over him. It was as though his arms, his legs, his body, were all . . . dissolving. He seemed to be falling and he couldn't even reach out his arms to grab at something as he went down into a great blazing pit of brilliant white light.

CHAPTER SEVEN
DILLINGER'S HAT

Kip's feet thudded against a hard surface. He felt like he was going to fall and had to fling out his arms in order to regain his balance. Then everything swam back into focus. He stood there, staring in complete astonishment at his surroundings, trying to understand what had just happened. But he couldn't really take it in. This was nuts.

He was standing on a street in the middle of a big city – but it wasn't a city in the modern day and it wasn't even the UK. It was a city he had seen recently. In *Public Enemy Number One*.

Now it came to him, pretty much the last thing that Mr Lazarus had said before pushing him into the light. 'I'll contact you when you're there and explain *everything*.' Kip stared around open-mouthed.

He could feel a sense of panic rising within him. He was in the film. He was really in the film!

The blare of a car horn almost made him jump out of his skin and he scuttled to one side, allowing a black Ford to rumble past him. He could see the driver staring at him through his side window, his mouth open as though he was looking at a spaceman.

Kip realised that his red T-shirt, jeans and Converse trainers must look strangely out of place here.

He looked around again. He couldn't stop himself. Everything was here in perfect detail – the cars, the people, the buildings. Glancing upwards, he saw a couple of dowdy pigeons flapping overhead. He had to take a deep breath and hold it for a moment, because he felt as though he was going to panic.

Then the phone-like thing on his hip started beeping loudly. He looked down at it in dull surprise and pulled it from its holster. A green button was flashing, so he pressed that and lifted the device to his ear.

'Well, Kip,' said Mr Lazarus's voice, compressed to a tiny insect-like buzz in Kip's ear. 'What do you think?'

'I . . . think . . . I must have . . . I can't . . . this can't be happening!'

'Oh, but it is, Kip. Look around you. It's all there in perfect detail.'

'But . . . it looks . . . real.'

'It *is* real. When you go into a film it becomes real. You mustn't forget that.'

'How do you mean, *real*?'

'I mean that Russell Raven is no longer an actor. He is John Dillinger, public enemy number one. His gang is real, his bullets are real. Get hit by one of those bullets and you could be killed.'

Kip actually pulled the brick-shaped gadget away from his ear and stared at it for a moment. Then he lifted it back.

'But that doesn't make sense. Russell Raven makes other films, so—'

'Yes, but he's not *physically* there. How can I explain it to you? He's left a kind of...ghost of himself trapped in the celluloid, his real self is off somewhere making new movies. But it's different for you, Kip. You're actually in this copy of the film, and you must be very careful. Listen to me. If it gets to the closing credits and you're still there, the film will claim you as its own. You'll be trapped there for ever.'

Kip allowed himself a brief smile.

'You're kidding, right?'

'I'm deadly serious. I would never joke about a thing like that.'

'Then you've got to get me out of here!' protested Kip. 'Right now. I've...got things to do in the real world. I...I have a homework assignment I'm supposed to complete over the holidays!'

Mr Lazarus laughed. 'Relax, Kip,' he said. 'Of course I'm going to get you out of there. But first, there's something I want you to do for me.'

'But—'

'Just do as I say. Firstly, I want you to turn round and start walking along the street. Keep the line of parked cars to your right. You have an appointment with Mr Dillinger in a very short time and I don't want you to miss it. Now hurry up, there isn't time to waste.'

Kip turned and began to walk along the street. His mind was racing and he kept the Communicator clamped to his ear.

'How...how does it work?' he asked. 'The Enigma, I mean.'

'I don't know.'

'What do you mean, you don't...?' Kip was interrupted by the roar of an engine and the shrieking of tyres. Looking over his shoulder in alarm, he could see that a group of black cars had just skidded to a halt a few yards behind him. Men were spilling out of them, tough-looking men, all of them carrying Tommy guns. They were advancing towards him, staring along the street as they came. Now Kip turned to follow their gaze, just in time to see a line of police cars pulling to a halt several hundred yards further up the road.

With a sinking feeling, he recalled the scene into which he had just wandered – a furious shoot-out between Dillinger's gang and the cops. Kip remembered that the police had set up blocks on all the roads south of the town – behind the gang. The only possibility of escape lay to the north, from where another group of armed cops were advancing. Kip was now trapped between Dillinger's gang and the police.

'Oh great,' he said.

'Kip?' buzzed Mr Lazarus's voice. 'Is something wrong?'

'Why did you send me into this scene? It's not—'

The sudden thunder of machine-gun fire made Kip wince. Several bullets whined past his head with a sound like angry wasps. It occurred to him that he was standing in a very dangerous place.

He spotted a gap between two parked cars and threw himself towards it, just as a series of shots rattled out on either side of him. He dropped gratefully down between the cars as bullets smashed windscreens and punched ragged holes in black bodywork all around him. The stink of cordite filled the air. He threw his hands over his head and lay where he was for a moment, trying to catch his breath.

He heard a kind of whining sound and realised that Mr Lazarus was speaking to him. He lifted the Communicator to his ear.

'You've got to tell me how to get out of here,' he gasped. 'They're shooting at me. I could be killed!'

'Don't be so melodramatic. You're under cover, aren't you? I saw you dive behind those cars.'

'How?'

'I'm watching on the screen, of course. Now. First things, first. Pull out the earpiece from the Communicator and press the HANDS FREE button. Then put the handset back in its holster. We'll still be able to talk and you'll have the use of your hands.' Kip examined the gadget. He could see a little earpiece fixed to one side of it and when he pulled gently on it, it unreeled from the handset on a length of wire. He took a couple of moments to get the thing pressed into his ear. Now Mr Lazarus's voice seemed to fill his head.

'All done?'

'Yes.'

'Excellent. Now, I want you to move towards the sidewalk and have a look up the street.'

Kip took a deep breath and did as he was told. He stuck his head carefully out from behind the rear bumper of the car ahead of him. Everything seemed clear. Mr Lazarus urged him on. 'I want you to move out from there, keeping under cover from the bullets and I want you to grab something for me.'

'Grab what?' asked Kip in exasperation.

'John Dillinger's hat.'

'His . . . his hat? What do you want that for?'

'It's not for me. A collector friend of mine wants it and he's willing to pay big money for it.'

Kip felt a sudden wave of disgust go through him.

'Is that what this is all about?' he cried. 'You're some kind of . . . thief?'

There was a brief pause, during which Kip imagined the old man's outraged expression.

'That's a very harsh word,' he said. 'You must remember, I'm just taking worthless film images. It's the Enigma that turns them into real objects. And besides, I have to fund myself in some way. I have devoted my life to rescuing cinemas across the world; I deserve a few creature comforts. I can't pay for those on the money your father pays me, can I?'

'Well . . .' said Kip.

'We're wasting time. Get out from behind that car and make your way up the sidewalk towards the police before it's too late.'

Kip crawled out from the gap and got onto his hands and knees. He began to creep along the line of parked cars, heading towards the cops – who he figured were at least less likely to shoot at him than the bad guys. But then he caught a movement out of the corner of his eye and, looking through a gap in the cars, he saw to his horror that a bad guy was standing in the road, staring back at him from beneath the brim of his hat. The man's face was cold and merciless and Kip saw that he was lifting his Tommy gun to fire.

'No!' yelled Kip. 'Hang on, I'm not supposed to—'

In that instant gunfire rattled from further up the street and the bad guy was blown backwards as a couple of shots thudded into his chest. As he fell, he lost his grip on the Tommy gun and it came skittering across the road between the gap in the cars. Kip grabbed at it instinctively, staying where he was for a moment, gasping for breath.

'What's going on?' asked Mr Lazarus in his ear.

'Didn't you see? A man was going to shoot me only—'

'The action has moved on,' said Mr Lazarus. 'Remember, I'm watching the edited version of events, but for you, it's all happening in real time.'

'Huh? I don't really—'

'You'll get used to it. Right now, the camera is following Mr Dillinger. He's somewhere behind you but I think he should go past you at any moment.'

As if to prove the theory, a figure raced past Kip; a man in a heavy overcoat and a wide-brimmed hat. He was holding a Tommy gun and racing fearlessly towards the cops up ahead of him. Kip realised with a dull sense of shock that it was Russell Raven. No, he corrected himself, not him at all. It was John Dillinger. He had his head down, he was running for all he was worth and firing as he ran.

'Wait!' yelled Kip, but Dillinger didn't seem to hear him. He kept right on going, his Tommy gun blazing.

'He's just run past me!' yelled Kip.

'Then get after him. We need that hat.'

Kip gritted his teeth, got to his feet and went grimly in pursuit. He had only gone a short distance when he became aware of somebody else running up the road alongside him. Risking a glance, he saw that another gangster was racing towards the police, firing his Tommy gun as he ran, swinging it from left to right to lay down a deadly hail of bullets. Kip recognised him as Baby Face Nelson, one of Dillinger's gang, a small man with a reputation as a cold-blooded killer.

And that was when Kip remembered a scene from the film, one of its most shocking moments. A young mother pushing a baby carriage, was caught in the crossfire and killed. He glanced further up the street and sure enough, there she was, cowering in the middle of the road, her face a picture of terror as Nelson ran towards her, ready to shoot her down.

There was no time to think. Kip lifted his own weapon, pointed it towards Nelson and pulled the trigger. The wooden stock thudded against his shoulder as he unleashed a flurry of bullets in Nelson's general direction. The gangster stopped firing and dived behind a car that had stopped in the middle of the street. Glass exploded from the car's windows as Kip's bullets peppered the vehicle and Nelson was obliged to duck down for cover. Kip glanced up the street and saw to his relief that the woman had taken the opportunity to push the pram to safety on the far side of the road, where she dived into a shop doorway.

Kip's gun gave a harsh click. He was out of bullets. He dropped the weapon and went after Dillinger again, running as fast as his legs would carry him. To his right, a shopkeeper shouted to him to get off the street but he ignored the advice, intent now on getting hold of what he had been sent in for; Dillinger's hat. Maybe if he got that, Mr Lazarus would tell him how to get out of here. As he closed in on his quarry, he wondered what he was supposed to do when he caught up with the gangster. He could hardly just ask him for it, could he? Dillinger was not known for his friendliness to random kids. The gangster came to an intersection and went around it, running for all he was worth. Kip went after him.

He turned the corner and saw to his horror that Dillinger had run into even bigger trouble. He was slowing down, looking left and right for some avenue of escape. More cops were advancing along the street, firing their guns at pretty much anything that moved. Kip renewed his efforts, closing the gap between him and Dillinger, horribly aware of bullets ricocheting up from the sidewalk around him. Then he saw the gangster drop to his knees behind a line of rubbish bins and start firing back at the cops. They scattered in all directions, but Dillinger kept shooting. His bullets ran out and he was obliged to pause so he could pull out the spent magazine and replace it with a new one. Sensing an opportunity, Kip ran forward, grabbed the brim of Dillinger's hat and whipped it off his head. For an instant Dillinger stopped what he was doing and looked up in surprise. He stared at Kip for a moment, his expression hostile. Then he relaxed and grinned. He reached up, grabbed Kip by one arm and pulled him down into cover.

'Keep your head down, kid!' he snapped. 'Where the hell did you come from?'

'You wouldn't believe me if I told you,' said Kip. A couple of bullets smacked into the far side of the bins, making him flinch. He lifted the hat. 'Is it OK if I take this?' he asked.

'A souvenir, huh?' muttered Dillinger. 'So you can boast to all your pals that you met public enemy number one?'

Kip nodded. 'Kind of,' he said.

'OK, kid, take it, I got plenty of others.' Dillinger risked a peek over the top of the rubbish bins. 'Doesn't look like I'm gonna be needing it, anyway,' he said. 'I reckon they've got me cornered.'

'Oh, don't worry,' said Kip. 'You escape from this. Some of your men will be along in a minute in a stolen police car.'

Dillinger gave him an odd look.

'How would you know that?' he growled.

'Oh, I saw the . . . I mean, I . . . it's . . . just a feeling.'

Dillinger slapped another magazine into his gun and lifted his head cautiously over the top of the bins to look up the street. The cops were creeping out from cover. He lifted the Tommy gun and unleashed a barrage of bullets at them, sending them running back again.

'I see you've got the hat,' said a voice in Kip's ear.

'Huh? Oh yes. Now how do I get out of here?'

Dillinger stopped firing for a moment. 'Who are you talking to?' he asked.

Kip ignored him. He was too busy listening to Mr Lazarus giving instructions.

'Remember the Retriever? The thing you are wearing around your neck?'

'Oh yeah, right.' Kip reached under his T-shirt and pulled the gadget out. 'Got it,' he said.

'Pull back the metal cover,' said Mr Lazarus. 'It's hinged. Underneath, you'll find a button marked EXIT. Press that.'

'OK,' cried Kip. 'As easy as that?'

'Yes. Hurry now, there isn't much time.'

'Who the hell are you talking to?' asked John Dillinger again.

Kip glanced at him. 'A friend,' he said. He jammed Dillinger's hat on his own head and tried to pull back the metal cover, but it was hard to open.

'What's that?' asked Dillinger.

'It's a . . . lucky charm,' said Kip.

64

'Yeah? Maybe you should lend it to me. I think I'm going to need it. Tell you what, I'll trade it for the hat.'

'Er... no, don't worry, your friends will be here any minute.'

'Think so? Those cops are getting awful... oh rats!' Dillinger suddenly leaped to his feet and started racing back the way he had come. 'Run, kid!' he yelled over his shoulder.

Kip was puzzled. He turned and peeped over the top of the bins.

A truck had been driving along the street alongside him, but now Kip could see that it was mounting the pavement and heading straight towards him. It was only now that he remembered the scene from the film. He caught a brief glimpse of a shattered windscreen and the driver slumped over his wheel, his face a mask of agony.

'Oh hell!' muttered Kip. He jumped to his feet and started to run after Dillinger, fumbling with the Retriever as he did so. The metal cover had a latch that just wouldn't seem to come undone. He heard a loud crash behind him as the truck's front bumper smashed into the bins and flung them in all directions... Desperately Kip forced his thumbnail under the Retriever's metal cover, revealing the EXIT button, which was pulsing with a dull red glow. Kip turned his head to look back.

Too late, he thought. The truck's metal grille was towering above him, only inches away and his head filled with the roar of an engine, his nostrils with the sharp stink of gasoline. In the same instant, his thumb closed on the button. For a horrible moment, absolutely nothing happened. Then he was melting again and a brilliant light filled his head, mingling with the fading roar of the truck's engine.

Suddenly, he was yanked backwards and he was crouched on the wooden platform, his arms held up to cover his face. He was back in the projection room and Mr Lazarus was smiling down at him.

'Nice job,' he said.

CHAPTER EIGHT

SAVED

Kip got unsteadily to his feet. He was shaking from head to foot.

'Good boy,' said Mr Lazarus. He lifted the hat gently from Kip's head. 'You've done very well. Quite the little action hero. I saw some of what happened on screen but, unfortunately, when Dillinger ran from the truck, the camera stayed with him.' He took Kip's arm and helped him down from the platform. Kip opened his mouth and tried to say something but for the moment he was speechless. 'Here, sit down a while,' suggested Mr Lazarus. He helped Kip over to a packing case and eased him in to a sitting position. 'Are you all right, my friend?' he asked. 'You seem a little . . . overwhelmed.'

'I . . . I was nearly *killed*,' whispered Kip.

'Really?' Mr Lazarus frowned. 'Well, I did warn you it could be dangerous.'

'There . . . there was this truck. It was coming straight at me.'

Mr Lazarus smiled and put the hat down carefully on a worktop, handling it as though it was some precious relic. 'The hat looks quite undamaged,' he observed. 'I was worried it might have been torn.'

Kip glared at him.

'Never mind about the bloody hat!' he snarled. 'What about me?'

'Oh, you're right as rain,' Mr Lazarus assured him. 'And please watch your language.' He turned back with a sly smile. 'So tell me, Kip. Wasn't it amazing?'

Kip nodded.

'Yes,' he admitted. 'It was incredible...but...did you have to send me into such a violent scene? I mean, there were bullets flying everywhere.'

Mr Lazarus shrugged. 'I just thought it was the part of the film where you had the best chance of getting the hat,' he said. He studied Kip for a moment. 'I suppose it *was* pretty intense.'

A thought occurred to Kip. 'Hang on a minute,' he said. 'How come you already had the film cued to that scene? It's...it's almost as though you *knew* I'd turn up today. As though you planned this.'

Mr Lazarus gave him a disapproving look.

'Kip, has anybody ever told you, you have a very suspicious nature?'

Kip frowned. He wasn't convinced for a moment but decided to change the subject. 'You were telling me before,' he said, 'about the Retriever.'

'Was I?'

'Yes, you were. You said that you didn't know how

it worked. But that doesn't make sense. You invented it, right?'

'Oh yes, back in the 1950s. To tell you the truth, I was trying to come up with an alternative to 3D... something that would rival the process without the need for those ridiculous cardboard glasses everyone was wearing. So I started experimenting with prisms. It was an accident, really. I wouldn't have known about it at all if it wasn't for Federico.'

Kip frowned. 'Who's Federico?' he muttered.

'My pet monkey, a constant companion back then. I was working at the Fantastique in Paris. Do you know it?'

'No. I suppose it's a cinema?'

'Of course.' Mr Lazarus smiled as though recalling happy memories. 'I had set up my equipment in the projection room and I was running a copy of *Invasion of the Body Snatchers* while I fiddled about with the prism. Federico just happened to wander into the beam of light. One moment he was there with me, the next he was up on the screen, being chased by an angry mob.'

'Wow! Did you... did you manage to get him out?'

'No. Oh, I wanted to, but I realised that if I just followed him in there, I wouldn't be able to get out myself. I needed to invent an escape device.' Mr Lazarus sighed. 'That took me years of

69

experimentation. And, when I was finally able to go into that copy of the film, I realised it was too late to rescue Federico. He'd been there till the closing credits, you see. The film even gave him his own credit. *Federico as Frightened Monkey.*' Mr Lazarus smiled a sad smile. 'I still have the original roll of film. I watch it sometimes just so I can see him. He seems happy enough. He is being chased by aliens, but they never quite manage to catch up with him.'

Kip shook his head.

'I've seen that film,' he said, 'and I don't remember a scene like that.'

'Of course not! It only affects the copy into which he was sent, and I made sure it never went back to the distributors. I told them it had been destroyed in an accident.' Mr Lazarus shrugged. 'So, that's how I came up with the Lazarus Enigma. I had invented an incredible machine. How it actually works doesn't really matter. It's what it *does* that counts.'

Kip nodded. 'It was the scariest thing that ever happened to me,' he said. 'And . . .'

'And what?' asked Mr Lazarus, moving a little closer.

'It was also kind of cool. I mean, everything was so real, every little detail. Not that I had much chance to study any of it. I was only in there for a few minutes. And if I'd been a couple of seconds slower pressing the exit button...' He shook his head. He didn't want to think about that.

'Hmm. Maybe next time, you'll be able to spend longer.'

'Next time?' Kip glared at Mr Lazarus. 'What makes you think there's going to be a "next time?"'

Mr Lazarus smiled.

'Because you said it was cool. And it *is* amazing, you have to admit.'

Kip had to think about that one. Somehow, he couldn't bring himself to lie about it.

'It could be great,' he admitted. 'Maybe if the film had been safer, a comedy or whatever, where the worst thing that could be thrown at you is a custard pie. *That* might be worth a go.'

Mr Lazarus smiled triumphantly.

'I *knew* you'd appreciate it,' he said. 'You've got cinema in your blood, Kip. The Lazarus Enigma was made for people like you. But we've got to make a deal, yes? The machine has to be our secret. You can't tell anybody else about it. Agreed?'

Kip nodded. 'There's no way I'd mention it to anyone,' he said. 'They'd think I'd lost the plot. Besides, if other people found out about what you've got there, who knows what could happen? There'd be idiots queuing up around the block wanting to go into a movie. We could probably charge admission...'

He saw Mr Lazarus's eyes widen as though this idea hadn't occurred to him.

'Oh no,' said Kip. 'No way! I want you to get a blanket and cover that thing up. If Dad ever found out about it, I don't know what he'd say.' The mention of his father made him look at his watch. 'I'd better get home,' he said. 'Dad will be wondering where I am.'

'You won't mention what happened today?'

'Are you kidding? I'm still not sure I believe it myself.'

He opened the door of the projection room and he and Mr Lazarus walked out into the empty auditorium.

'Kip. Aren't you forgetting something?'

'Hmm?'

'The Retriever. I need to put it somewhere safe.'

'Oh yeah, right.' Kip reached under his T-shirt and pulled out the device. He unhooked it from around his neck and looked at it for a moment, marvelling at how a piece of Perspex with a single button on it could have saved his life. Then he handed it to Mr Lazarus.

'And the Communicator,' Mr Lazarus reminded him.

Kip nodded. He unstrapped the leather holster and handed it over.

'Thank you, Kip.' Mr Lazarus slipped the Retriever

into his waistcoat pocket and slung the holster across his shoulder. 'I'll make sure everything's locked up before I leave,' he said.

Kip studied him for a moment.

'But you *don't* leave, do you?'

'Hmm?' Mr Lazarus attempted an innocent look, but it didn't quite come off.

'You live in the projection room,' said Kip. 'That's what the bed's for.'

Mr Lazarus smiled sheepishly.

'You are an observant boy,' he said. 'I would prefer it if you didn't mention this to your father.'

'Oh, I'll add it to the list,' said Kip. He unlocked the main doors and stepped out onto the street. He stood for a moment, blinking around in the unexpected sunlight. After his trip into *Public Enemy Number One*, even the ordinary looked somehow weird. He glanced up and down the road, half expecting to see a line of rickety black cars speeding towards him. But everything seemed normal. He shook his head and started walking back towards home. By the time he'd reached his street, his mind was whirring. He realised it was wrong, and probably crazy, but he was already putting together a list in his head; a list of the films he wouldn't mind making a brief appearance in.

CHAPTER NINE

ORIGINS

Kip couldn't stop himself from thinking back to his brief visit into the movie. It had all flashed by so quickly, he'd hardly had time to register what was happening to him. Now he thought that if the opportunity came up to visit a gentler, less dangerous film, he might just ask Mr Lazarus to send him in. How brilliant would it be to visit a fantastic world of science fiction? Or to spend a bit of time with one of his favourite movie stars, knowing that he had the Retriever with him to get him out of trouble if anything should go wrong? Mind you, the next scheduled film at the Paramount, *Terror Island*, wasn't the kind of movie he'd be in a great hurry to visit. If actors dressed as flesh-eating Neanderthals were going to turn into *real* flesh-eating Neanderthals, he frankly didn't want to be involved.

Still, it was something to think about for the future – and the more he thought about it, the more appealing it became. He even thought about telling Beth what had happened, but chickened out at the last minute, telling himself she'd think he'd lost it big time.

Meanwhile, Dad had started asking some awkward questions.

'Have you any idea where Mr Lazarus lives?' he asked Kip on Wednesday night, while they were waiting for the first customers to arrive.

'Er...no.' Kip could feel his face colouring. 'I've never asked.'

'Well, I have. I keep asking him for an address and phone number, just in case I need to get in touch with him, but every time I do, he finds some excuse not to give it to me. And...have you noticed how he's always the last to leave? He always seems to have a bit of fine-tuning to do up in that projection room.'

'It is great though, isn't it?' said Kip, desperate to change the subject. 'The Lazarus Enigma, I mean.'

'The what?'

'Er...that's what he calls the special equipment. As good as digital, I reckon.'

'Sounds like something out of a James Bond movie,' said Dad. 'But the results *are* amazing.' He'd watched the film on Monday night and, like everyone else, had been astonished by the quality of the image. 'It's weird,' he said. 'I mean, have you *looked* at that equipment?'

Kip played it cool.

'Yeah, I've glanced at it.'

'It's like something that's been put together in a garden shed. God knows how it does what it does.'

'It's an enigma,' said Kip, remembering something that Mr Lazarus had said to him. 'Hence the name.'

Dad gave him an odd look.

'I think you've been spending too much time with him,' he said. 'Now listen, Kip, I need to go home a little early tonight. Your Mum and I have some stuff we need to discuss.'

Kip shrugged his shoulders.

'No problem,' he said. 'I can sort out things here.'

'Thanks, Kip. I appreciate it.'

Dad headed home at about nine-thirty, leaving Kip to clear up. After the audience had gone, he went into the auditorium and did a quick check on the seats, throwing the worst of the rubbish into a black bin bag.

He was just finishing up when the door of the projection room opened and Mr Lazarus came out. He strolled down the steps to the centre of the cinema, his hands in the pockets of his fancy waistcoat.

'A good night, I think,' he said. 'The auditorium looked pretty full.'

'Best in ages,' Kip agreed. 'Dad was made up. By the way he was asking questions before. He says he needs an address from you.'

'He'll get one,' said Mr Lazarus.

'Yeah. Just so long as it's not, "The Projection Room, Paramount Picture Palace". I don't think he'd be too happy about that.'

'No, I don't suppose he would.' Mr Lazarus smiled. 'By the way, my collector friend was very pleased with John Dillinger's hat. It's going to take pride of place in his collection.' He lifted his gloved hand and a brown envelope appeared in it.

'How do you *do* that?' asked Kip.

'It's just a little bit of magic,' said Mr Lazarus. He handed the envelope to Kip. 'And that's a little something for your trouble.'

Kip opened it. It contained six crisp ten pound notes.

'Oh . . . I'm not sure I can take this,' he said.

'Why not? You earned it. Buy yourself something. Some new trainers, perhaps?'

Kip looked at Mr Lazarus. Only the previous day, he'd asked his mum about a new pair of trainers he'd seen online. The price? Sixty pounds.

'How do you do it?' he asked again.

'How do I do what?'

'Know stuff about people. And make things appear. And swap cheapo watches for nice expensive ones. Are you like a . . . magician, or something?'

Mr Lazarus smiled. 'It's as good a description as any. I think all projectionists are magicians. We take the stuff of dreams and we put them up there for all to see.' He gestured at the blank cinema screen.

Kip looked at the screen for a moment and then back at Mr Lazarus.

'I've got some more questions,' he said.

Mr Lazarus smiled. He ushered Kip into a seat and then took the one next to him. 'Fire away,' he suggested.

Kip frowned, not exactly sure what to ask first. Every question that appeared in his mind sounded stupid. Finally, he decided he had to start somewhere.

'Are you . . . are you *really* over a hundred years old?' he asked.

Mr Lazarus laughed.

'Hard ones first, eh?' He seemed to consider for a moment. 'I was born in 1890,' he said. 'In Naples.'

Kip did a quick calculation in his head.

'Flippin'eck!' he said.

Mr Lazarus seemed unperturbed.

'My father was a travelling salesman and my early years were spent moving from place to place. When I was around your age, we moved to Paris and it was while I was there that I first met the man who would influence my whole life. His name was Georges Méliès.'

'The film maker?' asked Kip.

Mr Lazarus looked at him, shocked. 'You have heard of him?' he gasped. 'I must say, I'm surprised. It was a very long time ago.'

'Well, I don't know much about him, but I read this article in a film magazine. It reckoned he was the father of science fiction.'

Mr Lazarus nodded.

'He has been called that. It's funny you mentioned magicians earlier because that is exactly what he did for a living before he discovered film-making. He taught me a few things.' Mr Lazarus lifted a hand and made a gesture. A white dove appeared in his palm and fluttered towards the roof of the cinema. Kip gazed up at it open-mouthed. Meanwhile, Mr Lazarus went right on talking. 'I was perhaps sixteen years old when I first went to his theatre and saw a film called *A Journey to the Moon...*' He paused for a moment. 'Do you still have my business card with you?'

Kip nodded. He reached into his back pocket and took it out.

'It's getting a bit creased,' he said.

'No matter.' Mr Lazarus drew the card between his thumb and forefinger and suddenly, it looked as though it had been freshly ironed. Then he tapped it once. Instantly, a grainy black and white image appeared on it – a round full moon, that appeared to be made from melting wax, floating in a black sky. The moon had a face, a jolly smiling face: the eyes moving, the lips pouting and smiling. The moon began to grow bigger as though a camera was tracking towards it. Then, quite suddenly, a huge bullet-shaped spaceship struck the moon and buried itself in the face's right eye. The moon's tongue came out of its mouth and it winced in pain. Then the image flickered and was gone.

'The most famous image from that film,' explained Mr Lazarus. 'Primitive by today's standards, but at the time, audiences were astounded. And I was in one such audience! Afterwards, I stayed behind and asked if I could speak to George. I told him that I was fascinated by what I had seen and I would very much like to work for him. He was kind enough to take me on as an apprentice at his studio and, in time, I became his chief projectionist.'

'But...' Kip was shaking his head. 'You couldn't be *that* old, could you? I mean, people of seventy and eighty are old wrecks. But you, you're well over a hundred and you don't look so bad.'

Mr Lazarus smiled. 'I will take that as a compliment,' he said. He went back to his little history. 'In nineteen-thirteen, George's company was put out of business by other, bigger film-makers and he could no longer employ me. I went to Venice, where I met Señor Ravelli, who was planning to open Il Fantoccini and I worked for him until nineteen thirty-five, when the floods finally closed his cinema. After that, it was Paris and La Fantastique. It was while I was working there that I created the Lazarus Enigma and began to understand all the amazing things it could do. I was in my early sixties by then. After that, I travelled the world, looking for cinemas that needed help – cinemas like the Paramount.'

'So...you didn't really come here from Venice?'

Mr Lazarus shook his head.

'I thought that sounded more impressive. Most recently I was working in a little cinema on a remote Scottish island. The Moonlight, a beautiful little place with seating for just thirty-five people. But that closed down a year ago. The owner died and the man who purchased it turned it into' – his lip curled – 'a pub.' He shook his head. 'Since then, I have simply been...waiting.'

'And how did you find out about us?'

'I have developed a sense. Cinemas in trouble, they draw me, just as a moth is drawn to a candle flame. I have to go to them and help them to survive.'

Kip frowned.

'It still doesn't explain the age thing,' he said. 'Come on, you have to admit, you don't look...' Kip did some quick maths in his head. '...over a hundred and twenty years old! I mean, that's mental!'

Mr Lazarus nodded.

'It is the Enigma that keeps me young. Among its many special properties, it has the ability to take a man's lines and wrinkles, all his infirmities, and lock them away in a piece of film. I always carry that reel of film around with me. Every so often, when I feel the years weighing heavy on my bones, I put myself into that film and when I come out again, I am restored to my former vigour. In the film there is an image of me as I should look now.' He seemed to shudder. 'It is not a pretty picture.'

'So . . . that's when you use the Retriever? To get back out again.'

'Correct. And, of course, I have to keep that film in a very safe place. If anything ever happened to it, I fear all the age that I have shed over the years would come back to visit me. And then I would be a . . . how did you describe it? Ah yes. An old wreck. But listen, Kip, I have told you all this in the strictest confidence. I do not want you to share this inform-ation with anybody else. Not your friends, not your family, do you understand?'

'Sure. You can count on me.'

'Good boy.' Mr Lazarus patted Kip on the shoulder. 'Now I think it is time you went home. Your parents will be wondering what has happened to you.'

Kip nodded. He slipped the business card into his back pocket and started to get out of his seat – but then he paused for a moment.

'That "staying young" thing,' he said. 'Would it work on anybody?'

'I don't know,' said Mr Lazarus. 'I never tried it on anyone else. But why would you be so interested? You're a young fellow, Kip; you have your whole life ahead of you.'

'Yeah. But I was just thinking. Sounds kind of cool.' He studied Mr Lazarus for a moment. 'Does it mean that you can live for ever?'

Mr Lazarus smiled sadly. 'Nobody lives for ever,' he said.

Kip frowned. 'Well, I'd better get home. Will you be OK to lock up?'

'Of course. I'll see you tomorrow.'

Kip headed for the exit, but glancing back he saw that Mr Lazarus was still in his seat. He was gazing up at the big, empty screen in front of him, as though watching a film of his very own.

A sudden thought flashed through Kip's mind.

That man is over one hundred and twenty years old.

Crazy as it sounded, Kip knew with a terrible certainty that it was absolutely true.

CHAPTER TEN

THE DEAL

'But I don't want to go to the cinema!' protested Rose, dragging back on Kip and Dad's hands. 'It's a rotten monster movie and I hate scary films.'

'But you won't even be watching it!' Kip reminded her. 'Why do you have to make everything so difficult?'

'We've brought your books and crayons,' added Dad. 'You can just sit in the office with me and amuse yourself.'

'It's not fair! Why do I have to?'

Kip sighed. It was Friday night and Mum had announced that she had yet another of her late meetings, which meant that he and Dad were stuck with Rose for the night.

'Why don't you ever get nice films?' she demanded. 'Something *I'd* like to watch. Something about ponies or fairies or princesses?'

'We *do* get nice films sometimes,' Kip told her. 'But we can't do anything about tonight. Anyway, it's Dad who chooses the films, not me.'

This was true – though, in reality, Kip was a big influence on Dad's choices.

'They don't make many nice films any more,' said Dad. 'Most people prefer the scary ones.'

'Well I don't!'

'It's only for a couple of hours,' Kip reminded her. 'You'll be able to sit in the office and draw. You *like* drawing.'

Rose looked at him indignantly.

'I have to be in the mood,' she told him.

The Paramount came in to view and they saw Mr Lazarus waiting by the open doors. He smiled at Rose as Kip dragged her up the steps and inside.

'Ah, here's my favourite girl,' he said. 'How are you tonight, Rose?'

'All right,' said Rose, grumpily. She always seemed very wary of Mr Lazarus, Kip thought, but she was like that with most people until she got to know them properly. It came from years of Mum telling her not to have anything to do with strangers. And they didn't come much stranger than Mr Lazarus.

Just then, Dad's mobile phone rang. He lifted it to his ear and listened for a moment. His expression became grave.

'Oh no,' he said. Kip looked at him. 'Oh dear,' he said. 'I see. Well, of course somebody needs to be there with her. Uh huh. Just a minute.' He took the phone away from his ear and looked at Kip. 'It's Grannie,' he said. 'She's had a bit of a fall. Nothing too serious but they've taken her into hospital. They're going to have to operate tonight.' Kip knew that this was a big problem. Grannie lived alone in a little house in Blackburn and had nobody up there who could help her. Dad thought for a moment, clearly unsure of what to do. 'I won't be able to contact your mum; she always switches her mobile off in meetings . . . but somebody needs to go over to Blackburn and help sort Grannie out.' He looked at Kip and Mr Lazarus. 'I'm afraid we might have to cancel the film for tonight.'

Kip stared at his father. 'We can't do that!' he protested. 'It's the first night of *Terror Island*. The place will be packed.'

'I can't help that. It's hard enough running things with three people, let alone two. And there's Rose to think about.'

Mr Lazarus stepped forward and placed a hand reassuringly on Dad's shoulder.

'Please don't worry, Mr McCall,' he said. 'We can handle things here, can't we, Kip?'

'Er . . . yeah, sure, absolutely.' Kip nodded. 'Course we can.'

'Kip can handle the ticket booth and the confectionary and I can move between the projection room and the office. Once the film is running, I'll be free to come down and help Kip out.

'I don't know . . .' said Dad. 'It's a bit of a tall order.'

'Not at all. You just go and do whatever you need to do.' Mr Lazarus smiled that sleepy smile of his. 'We'll take care of everything. I promise.'

Dad still looked worried but lifted the phone to his ear again. 'OK, tell her I'm on my way,' he said. 'I'll be there as soon as I can.' He rang off. 'OK, Kip, obviously you'll have to keep a close eye on Rose tonight.'

'Oh but, Dad, it's Friday. It's—'

'I know what night it is,' Dad assured him. 'But just for once you're going to have to give the movie a miss. You'll be able to catch up with it any other night this week.'

'But, Dad—'

'No buts, Kip. This is an emergency and I'm counting on you.' Dad turned and hurried towards the entrance doors. 'I should be back by the end of the film,' he called over his shoulder. 'If you have any problems, ring me.' And then he was gone, hurrying back in the direction of the house to collect his car.

Kip stood there, his mouth open. This couldn't be happening. Not on a Friday night! Not for the opening of *Terror Island*!

With a sigh, he led Rose through into the ticket office and began to unpack her things onto Dad's desk: books, crayons, her favourite toys. She watched impassively as he set everything out for her.

'You'll be fine,' Kip told her.

'I'll be *bored*,' she insisted.

'Please, Rose, help me out here. Do some colouring in or something.'

He went through to the confectionary booth and switched on the popcorn maker. Mr Lazarus followed him.

'You have fully recovered from your little trip in to the world of film?' murmured Mr Lazarus.

Kip glanced towards the open door, hoping that Rose wasn't listening – but she seemed totally intent on playing with her toys.

'I guess,' said Kip. 'Looking back, it seems like something I dreamed.'

'It *is* incredible,' said Mr Lazarus. 'What you youngsters call "mind-blowing." But, of course, you were only in there for a few minutes. Next time, we'll have to see if we can't put you in for a little longer.'

Kip looked at him incredulously. 'I already told you, there's not going to be a next time.'

'You said that. But don't tell me you haven't thought about it.'

'Yeah, I've *thought* about it. But I don't know… it would have to be a safe film. Definitely not something like *Terror Island*. I really don't fancy getting chewed up by a sabre-toothed tiger, thanks very much.'

Mr Lazarus nodded.

'I can see why you'd be nervous about that,' he admitted. 'It isn't the most appealing idea. But listen,

I spent some time last night making a few adjustments to the Retriever. I think it's even better than it was. It's my belief that it might now be possible to bring a live character *out* of the film.'

Kip stared at him.

'But . . . I thought you said that if you were there when the credits rolled, you couldn't ever get out.'

'That's true of *real* people, like you and me. But film characters are different. You remember I told you they're like ghosts of themselves? I think now the prism could actually give those ghosts solid form. It's very exciting.'

'Look, could we talk about this another time?' hissed Kip, glancing nervously towards the open office door.

'Oh yes, of course. Point taken.'

'And listen,' added Kip. 'You *have* covered up the equipment, right?'

'I've thrown a sheet over it. At least, over the parts I don't use to improve the film image. And don't worry, I won't remove it again, not unless you ask me to.'

'Don't hold your breath,' Kip told him.

The entrance doors opened and Beth stepped into the foyer. She came over to Kip and smiled, but when the smile wasn't returned, she sensed that something was different tonight. She watched as he glumly filled a box with popcorn.

'Problem?' she asked.

'Yeah. Grannie's had a fall, Dad's had to shoot off to Blackburn and now I'm going to have to miss the film so I can keep an eye on Rose.'

Beth frowned. 'Oh, that's a pain,' she said. 'Can't we talk her into watching the film with us? It's only a twelve A.'

'No you can't!' said Rose's voice from the office.

Beth smiled.

'There's nothing wrong with *her* hearing,' she observed.

'No,' said Kip, nervously, thinking about what he and Mr Lazarus had just been discussing. 'Anyway, there's nothing I can do about it. I'll be stuck out here.'

'Maybe there's a solution,' said Mr Lazarus. 'How about if Rose brings her crayons and things up to the projection room?'

Kip looked at him. 'Seriously?' he asked.

'Why not?' Mr Lazarus looked towards the door of the office and raised his voice a little. 'I'm sure Rose would like to see how the projector works,' he said.

There was a brief pause and then Rose's voice said, 'Whatever.'

'But what about the ticket booth? Somebody might come late.'

'Not to worry. At eight o'clock, I'll set the film running, then I'll come down and keep an eye on the booth for half an hour or so. Once I'm sure nobody else is coming, I'll go back up to the projection room to see how Rose is getting on. Easy.'

'I'm not sure,' said Kip.

'Oh, go on,' Beth urged him. 'She'll be safe up in the projection room.'

Kip thought about it for a moment and then nodded. 'OK, that'd be great,' he said. 'Thanks, Mr Lazarus.' He grinned at Beth and reached into the fridge for her Diet Coke. 'In that case, save me a seat,' he said. 'And don't hang about. I've got a feeling we're going to be very busy tonight.'

He was right. What started as a trickle soon became a flood. It seemed that news of the Paramount's fabulous new projection system was getting around, because there were faces in tonight that Kip had never seen here before, and a lot of money seemed to be changing hands. He was kept very busy, running from ticket office to confectionary booth and back again. He seemed to be doling out huge amounts of popcorn, drinks and sweets, and he told himself that Dad would be well impressed when Kip presented him with the takings after he got back from the hospital.

The last few ticket holders drifted into the auditorium as the clock inched towards ten minutes past the hour and right on cue Mr Lazarus appeared in the door of the ticket booth.

'I've just set the film running,' he announced.

'OK. How's Rose?'

'She's fine. Playing with her toys.' Mr Lazarus raised a gloved hand and suddenly it was holding a large container full of hot popcorn. He handed it to Kip. 'Hurry along now,' he said. 'Or you'll miss the start of the film. I don't know about you, but to my mind that's the worst thing that can ever happen.'

Kip nodded. He couldn't agree more.

'Thanks, Mr Lazarus,' he said. 'I owe you one.'

He hurried out of the booth, pushed through the doors and climbed the flight of steps to the auditorium. Eerie theme music was playing and, as he descended the steps to the stalls, he saw the title *Terror Island* scrawled across the screen in blood-red letters. He dropped into the vacant seat that Beth had saved for him and settled down to watch the movie.

CHAPTER ELEVEN

COMPLICATIONS

Rose was bored. She'd coloured in almost half a picture in her *Flying Fairies* book and there was absolutely nothing else of interest in the projection room. She looked forlornly around, wondering when Mr Lazarus was coming back. He had said he'd only be gone a minute or so.

Rose decided that there was something very strange about Mr Lazarus. She remembered that, a little while earlier, she'd overheard him and Kip in the confectionary booth. The two of them had been whispering about something... something that had to do with equipment that was stored up here in the projection room. Kip had warned Mr Lazarus to keep it covered up. Now Rose was beginning to wonder what they had been talking about...

She got up from her chair and standing on tiptoe, she peeped through the little window into the auditorium. For the moment, things didn't seem too bad. A bunch of Americans were aboard a boat and they were arguing about something.

'*And I'm telling you, there's no island on any of my charts!*' shouted a man who seemed to be in charge of things. *'I've been sailing these waters for years; if there was an island out here, I'd know about it.'* He was tall and powerful-looking and wore a scuffed-leather jacket. He talked in a kind of growl, gritting his teeth as he spoke. A pretty blonde woman seemed to be leading an argument against him.

'And I'm telling you, Captain Holder, that I have documents going back hundreds of years that testify to the existence of such an island. The ancient tribes called it "The place of the monsters!"'

That was enough for Rose. She could not for the life of her understand why anybody would want to watch a scary film. She turned back from the window and her attention was caught by something beside the projector – something that was covered by a big black sheet.

Down at the front, Kip was enjoying the film. This part was known as 'the set-up' and he knew that it was important to get the first half-hour right, in order for the audience to accept all the fantastical things that would follow.

The blonde actress, Kara Neetly, was playing Dr Tamara Flyte, an anthropologist (whatever that was). She had chartered a yacht belonging to Captain Dash Holder – played by tough-guy actor Clint Westwood – and ordered him to take her and her team of two scientists out to look for a mysterious island that she'd been reading about for years. But Captain Holder was convinced that all the old stories were just a bunch of myths and that there was nothing out here but 'more water'. It was night time and they'd been searching for ten days now, without success. They had all gathered in the cabin for an emergency meeting.

'This is a wild-goose chase,' growled Captain Holder. 'I don't know why I ever agreed to this trip.' His deep snarling voice made him sound like he was permanently constipated.

'But you *did* agree to it,' said Dr Flyte. 'And as long as I'm paying your wages, you'll do as I say.'

'No way, lady. It's over when I say it's over.'

The rest of the team looked on in anxious silence. They comprised of Tad Baxter, a young research assistant who wore his hair long and spent all his time cracking bad jokes, and Jade Callahan, a pretty brunette who seemed to take every opportunity to wear as few clothes as possible.

The film cut to a long shot of the yacht ploughing through the water. It was late afternoon, the sun very low on the horizon. Captain Holder's first mate, Sam, an elderly man in a yellow raincoat, stood at the tiller, helping himself to gulps of whiskey from a hip flask. He wasn't taking very much notice of what was going on around him – but the ominous music that was slowly building to a climax was enough to tell Kip that something bad was about to happen.

Rose reached up on tiptoe to pull the sheet aside. It fell away, revealing an odd-looking piece of machinery, which seemed to consist of a round wooden platform on a set of metal rails. There was also a funny-shaped lump of glass on an upright pole. She wondered if this was what Kip and Mr Lazarus had been talking about.

She reached out a hand to touch the round wooden thing and it moved under her fingers, gliding smoothly forward an inch or so. She stopped it and pulled it back a little, gazing at it with interest. She noticed the marks of a couple of footprints on the pale wood and guessed that you were supposed to stand on it. She pushed it gently forward, to see if anything would happen. Almost immediately, a beam of light was reflected into the glass shape and this angled sharply down to illuminate the platform with a fierce white glare. She pulled it back again and stared at it for a moment, trying to puzzle out what it did. She wasn't sure why, but she thought that a person was supposed to stand on the platform and then slide forward into the light, though she couldn't see any point in actually doing it. *Perhaps*, she thought, *it would make her look like a dancer in a spotlight, the kind of thing she liked to watch on TV.*

Why not try it, slide into the light and take a bow? After all, what harm could it do? She thought for a moment and then came to a decision.

She climbed up onto the platform.

On screen, Captain Holder was still arguing with Tamara Flyte.

'Doctor Flyte, I'd appreciate it if you'd stick to what you know and leave the handling of the ship to me,' he said.

'I'm not trying to interfere,' Dr Flyte assured him. 'I just want to be sure we haven't missed anything. If you'd just read the articles I've collected about this mysterious island, I feel sure that...'

'We'll give it one more day,' said Captain Holder. 'If we don't find anything by then, we'll have to—'

He broke off at a sudden crashing sound and everybody was thrown violently sideways. Captain Holder threw out his hands to a nearby table to steady himself. He stared around, a look of anger on his grizzled face. 'What in the name of God was that?' he roared.

Rose stood for a moment, wondering what to do next.

After a few moments, she decided that she needed to get the platform to move forward again, so it would slide into the light. She tried rocking backwards and forward on her feet, but that did nothing. Then she realised she would have to do it as though she was on her scooter. She dropped one foot to the floor and kicked herself off. That did the trick. The platform slid smoothly forward a second time and in an instant the powerful light was blazing into her eyes, a light so strong that she had to lift a hand to protect them. And then she began to feel very, very strange indeed . . .

On screen, the characters were now scrambling up the steps to the deck, only to find that the yacht had beached itself on a sharp coral reef and was sticking up from the water at a crazy angle. Captain Holder looked over the side and saw that water was pouring into the yacht through a jagged hole in the hull. Sam was staggering around the deck shouting that they'd run aground, which Kip thought was a bit rich, since it wouldn't have happened in the first place if he'd kept a proper eye on things.

'Look!' cried Tamara. She was pointing to the horizon where everyone could see the distant outline of a tropical island silhouetted against a brilliant red sunset. 'What did I tell you?' she cried, as she spun round to confront the captain. 'There *is* an island.'

'Lucky for us,' snarled Captain Holder, 'because this ship is going down, fast.' He swung round. 'Sam, unhitch the lifeboat. We don't have much time.'

'Aye aye, Captain,' spluttered Sam, pushing the hip flask back into his pocket out of sight.

'Wait!' cried Tamara. 'My charts! My equipment!'

'Forget them,' roared Captain Holder. 'We've got to—'

He broke off in amazement as a little girl appeared on the deck right in front of him. He stared down at her in wide-mouthed amazement. 'Where the hell did you come from?' he gasped.

The girl looked up at him, her hands on her hips, her expression very cross indeed.

'What's going on?' she screamed. 'How did I end up here?'

Down in his seat, Kip had just been taking a sip from Beth's Coke but now he sprayed it all out with a gasp of horror. *Rose was in the film!* He sat there, his heart going twenty to the dozen, a horrible heat rising in his face. Beside him, he heard Beth say, 'Kip, that little girl. She looks just like—'

And then Kip was scrambling up out of his seat in a panic.

'Where are you going?' asked Beth. 'You'll miss the film.'

Kip ignored her. He began to run up the central aisle, heading for the steps that led up to the projection room. As he ran, he could hear the characters' voices booming from the cinema's sound system.

'Who the hell are you?' gasped Captain Holder.

'My name's Rose! How did I get here? I'm not supposed to be here. I *hate* scary movies!'

Uncertain laughter rippled through the audience.

Kip got to the door of the projection room and went inside. It was only then that he realised that Beth had followed him, but there was no time to worry about that now. The first thing he saw was the black sheet lying beside the Lazarus Enigma and the bright pool of light illuminating the wooden platform. He threw his hands to his face and went down on his knees.

'Oh no,' he gasped. 'Oh no, not Rose!'

Beth stood there staring at him.

'What's going on?' she asked anxiously. 'That kid in the film... she looks exactly like Rose.'

'It *is* Rose,' groaned Kip. 'Oh God... what am I going to say to Mum and Dad when they get back?'

Beth's face was a picture of astonishment.

'What do you mean?' she muttered. 'How *can* it be Rose? She's in here.' She looked around the darkened room. 'Isn't she?'

The door behind them swung open and Mr Lazarus stepped into the room. He stood there a moment, staring at Kip and Beth in surprise.

'What are you two doing up here?' he cried. 'You're missing the film.'

He noted the angry glare in Kip's eyes and then his own gaze moved sideways to look at the wooden platform, bathed in the light of the projector. The smile on his face faded in an instant.

'What's going on?' he asked blearily. 'Where's Rose?'

At that moment, Kip could have cheerfully strangled the old man.

'What have you done?' he whispered. 'For God's sake, she's only six years old.'

Mr Lazarus arranged his face into a look of total innocence.

'I haven't done anything,' he said. 'I was down in the ticket booth, taking care of a few stragglers.' He took a couple of steps closer to the projector and stared down at the wooden platform. 'Oh dear,' he said. 'How very unfortunate.'

CHAPTER TWELVE
THAT SINKING FEELING

Rose was feeling bewildered and rather scared. She gazed down over the rail of the sinking ship as the other members of the crew lowered a lifeboat into the churning waters. In the fading light, the sea appeared to be almost black. Captain Holder stared down at her for a moment and then strode away, shouting orders to the others.

Now the blonde-haired woman, who Rose recognised from the bit of film she'd watched earlier, came over to stand beside her. She was looking at Rose as though she didn't quite understand what she was doing here, but Rose felt exactly the same way about it. She understood she had somehow gone into the film but she didn't have the first idea how she was going to get out again.

'Where've you been hiding all this time?' asked the woman. She had an American accent. 'Are you a stowaway?'

Rose looked up at her.

'What's a stow...?'

'A stowaway,' said the woman, 'is somebody who hides aboard a ship.'

Rose shook her head. 'Haven't been hiding,' she protested. 'One moment I was at the Paramount, the next there was this light in my eyes and I was here.'

'You . . . were at the . . . Paramount?' The woman looked baffled. 'What does that mean exactly?'

'My dad has a cinema.'

'That must be very nice for you,' murmured the woman. 'But what does it have to do with anything?'

'I don't know. I was up in the room where they show the films and there was this black cloth and I took it off and . . .' Rose shook her head. 'I want to go home,' she said.

'We all want to go home, honey,' said the woman and slipped an arm round Rose's shoulders. 'But we can't right now.' She pointed to the horizon. 'First of all, we need to get to that island.'

Rose looked where the woman was pointing and sure enough, there on the blood-red horizon was a smudge of land, and what looked like a stretch of palm trees.

'Is this like a dream?' she asked.

'More of a nightmare,' said the woman grimly. As she said this, the deck of the ship seemed to lurch to one side and they had to grab hold of the rail to stop themselves from falling.

'I don't like this,' said Rose.

'You and me both, honey. What's your name?'

'Rose.'

'OK, Rose. I'm Doctor Tamara Flyte. Don't worry, I'm going to take real good care of you.'

Rose studied the woman for a moment.

'I've seen you before,' she said. 'You were in the trailer.'

Tamara looked confused.

'I don't live in a trailer, I have a very nice apartment.'

'No, the trailer for that horrible film!'

'You must be mixed up,' said Tamara. 'I'm not in films. I'm an anthropologist.'

'What's that?' asked Rose.

Tamara thought for a moment and then looked even more puzzled.

'I'm . . . I'm not really sure,' she said. 'But I know I *am* one.'

Just at that moment, the lifeboat dropped from its harness into the water with an almighty splash. Captain Holder came running along the deck towards them.

'Everybody into the boat!' he yelled. 'There's not much time. We're going down like a lead balloon.' As if to confirm this, the yacht gave a grinding roar and seemed to settle even lower in the water. 'She's slipping off the reef,' bellowed Captain Holder.

'Come on,' urged Tamara. She climbed over the rail and then turned back to hoist Rose up beside her. She was a lot stronger than she looked.

She pointed to a series of metal rungs on the ship's hull. 'Now we have to climb down,' she said. 'Think you can do that?'

Rose nodded. She hooked a leg over the metal rail and climbed down into the boat. When Rose was safely aboard, Tamara started coming down the rungs herself. She dropped the last few feet, making the boat wallow in the water.

'Be careful!' Rose chided her. 'You'll turn us over.'

'Sorry.' Tamara put her arm protectively around Rose and the two of them sank onto a padded bench on one side of the boat. Now another person was coming down the rungs, while Captain Holder shouted at him to hurry. He seemed to be doing an awful lot of shouting. A young man with long hair and horn-rimmed glasses dropped into the boat and settled himself down opposite Rose and Tamara.

'Where did the kid come from?' he asked.

'I don't know, Tad,' Tamara told him. 'She was . . .'

'There was a bright light and then I was here,' said Rose, trying to be helpful.

'Interesting,' said Tad. 'Sounds like some kind of teleportation.' He smiled at Rose. 'I'm Tad Baxter,' he said. 'Were you sent here from the island?'

'No, I was in the pictures,' said Rose.

'Pictures?' asked Tad. 'You mean like . . . paintings?'

Rose glared at him.

'No, I mean like a cinema.'

'A cinema?' Tad looked around at the raging sea all around them, then glared at Tamara. 'There's a cinema on the boat? How come nobody told me?'

'You're stupid,' said Rose, and Tad looked offended.

A slim, dark-haired woman who was wearing a halterneck and a pair of skimpy denim shorts climbed down into the boat too. She had a rucksack over one shoulder, from which several rolls of paper stuck out.

'I managed to grab some of your charts before the cabin flooded,' she told Tamara. 'And I sent out a distress call on the radio. Somebody might hear it and come looking for us.'

'Good work, Jade. Er… this is Rose.'

Jade dropped into a seat beside Rose. She looked at Tamara in surprise.

'Well, you sure kept *her* quiet,' she said.

'Oh, she's not mine,' protested Tamara. 'She just kind of… turned up.'

'Then I guess she's a stowaway,' said Jade.

'I'm *not* a stowaway,' said Rose, irritably. 'Why does everyone keep saying that? I don't know how I got here; I just know I want to go home.'

'Where *is* home?' asked Tamara, trying to be helpful.

'Forty-two, Napier Road,' said Rose and thought for a moment. 'I can't remember the postcode.' Tamara and Jade gave each other baffled looks.

'You mean the zip code?' asked Jade.

'I think postcodes are from the UK,' said Tamara. 'And her accent sounds kind of English to me.'

Captain Holder was the last to descend the ladder. He jumped into the boat and glared at a grizzled old man in a yellow raincoat, who was slumped in the prow. 'Nice job, Sam,' he growled.

'Captain, I had no chance, so I didn't,' shouted Sam. He sounded Irish or Scottish, Rose thought. Or perhaps even an American who was *trying* to sound Irish or Scottish. 'That blasted reef just came out of nowhere, so it did.'

'I'd be more convinced if I couldn't smell the whiskey fumes on your breath,' snarled Captain Holder. 'When we've got more time, you and me are gonna have a little talk about this.' He moved to the outboard motor and pulled a length of cord. It took a couple of attempts to get going but then the engine fired up and they started moving forward. 'Keep your eyes peeled for more reefs!' he yelled to the people in the prow. The boat had only moved off a short distance when the yacht gave a last convulsive shudder and began to slip beneath the waves. Captain Holder stood there, watching in silence as his ship sank to the bottom of the ocean. For a few moments, the masts still stuck up from the swaying surface of the water, but then they too were gone.

'I'm sorry, Captain,' blubbered Sam. 'She was a fine ship, so she was.'

'She was my dad's ship,' said Captain Holder. 'He managed to sail her for thirty years without a serious incident. Now she's gone.' He lowered his head for a moment and Rose thought that he might be about to burst into tears – but then he seemed to make a huge effort and snapped round to look at Tamara. 'Well, Doctor Flyte, looks like we found your mysterious island, after all. Let's just hope it's worth the price we paid to get here.'

Rose gazed ahead at the gradually approaching outline of the island, silhouetted against a blood-red sunset. Once again, she was reminded of the horrible trailer she had seen, last week. Hadn't there been a view of the same island in that? Wasn't this the island where the monsters lived?

'We can't go there,' she told Tamara, pointing.

'What do you mean, honey? We have to.'

'It's a bad place,' said Rose. 'There are horrible things there. Monsters.'

Tamara looked intrigued.

'But how could you know that?' she asked. 'Have you been there before?'

'No, but I've *seen* it.'

'Fascinating,' said Tad. 'Sounds like some kind of clairvoyance.'

Everyone ignored him.

'Well, whatever you think of the place, we have to go there,' said Tamara. 'We just don't have any other choice.'

108

The boat continued on its way towards the distant island.

'Let me get this straight,' said Beth. 'You're saying that Mr Lazarus can put people into films?'

'Yes,' said Kip. He was gazing through the hatch at the screen, where he could see Rose crammed into a lifeboat with the rest of the yacht's passengers. She looked pretty scared, which was understandable.

'You mean, like, *really* put them in?'

'Yeah. I went into one myself. *Public Enemy Number One*. It wasn't for long, but I was in it, all right.'

Beth stared at him enviously.

'Wow!' she said. 'That must have been brilliant.'

'It wasn't,' Kip told her. 'It was scary. I was nearly killed.'

'But, how? It's just a film, right?'

'It's complicated,' said Kip, tearing himself away from the hatch. He glared at Mr Lazarus. 'I'm going to have to go in and get her, aren't I?' he said.

Mr Lazarus frowned. 'I'm afraid so,' he said. 'I can't think of any other way of doing it. Still, at least it will give us a chance to try out the modifications I made to the Retriever.'

'Oh, that's fine then,' said Kip. 'So long as it's not all bad news.' He ran his hands through his hair. 'I don't believe this,' he said. 'Rose hates films like *Terror Island*. She'll be scared out of her wits.'

109

He looked apprehensively at the wooden platform. 'Should I go in now?'

Mr Lazarus frowned.

'I'm afraid you'll have to,' he said. 'Time *is* rather pressing.'

Beth frowned.

'But won't people in the audience recognise you?' she asked. 'Maybe you should wait until the audience have gone home and then run the film again.'

'We can't do that,' said Mr Lazarus. 'If she's still there when the closing credits roll, she's there for ever.'

Kip scowled. 'Just tell me you didn't plan this,' he said.

'Of course I didn't plan it! Kip, what do you take me for? I wouldn't put somebody into a film who didn't ask to go there.'

'I didn't ask to go in,' Kip reminded him.

'You didn't exactly protest, either.'

'Yes, but I didn't even know what was going to happen, did I? You tricked me and then you wouldn't let me out until I'd nicked John Dillinger's hat.'

'Whoah, hold on a minute!' said Beth. 'You nicked John Dillinger's hat?'

'Yeah,' Kip told her. 'Oh, don't worry. It's just this thing that Mr Lazarus does. Gets kids to steal stuff for him.'

110

'But you make me sound like a criminal!' protested Mr Lazarus. He looked at Beth imploringly. 'It's a little sideline I have. Absolutely harmless. And I only ask children to do it occasionally. *Special* children. Children who love cinema.'

Kip turned back to look through the hatch. Now the lifeboat was approaching a stretch of deserted beach. He turned away again. 'I can't stand this,' he said. 'I want to watch it, but I daren't. What if something bad happens to Rose?'

'Try not to worry about it,' Mr Lazarus assured him. 'I have faith in you, Kip. I'm sure you'll get to her before she's—'

'Before she's what?' cried Kip. '*Eaten?*'

'Oh, I'm sure it won't come to that,' said Mr Lazarus. 'But then, I suppose we have to be realistic. It *is* a monster movie.'

'Hold on a minute,' said Beth. 'You're saying that Rose could get properly eaten? Like, really chewed up and swallowed?'

Mr Lazarus looked slightly nauseated.

'Not the nicest way of putting it,' he said. 'But yes, when you are in the film, it's all real. Everything.'

'Wow,' said Beth. 'That's cool.' She looked at Kip. 'Right,' she said. 'I'm coming with you.'

'No way! I don't want you getting mixed up in this.'

'Can't be helped. There's no way I'm going to let my boyfriend go to Terror Island without being there to back him up.'

Kip stared at her.

'Since when have I been your boyfriend?' he cried.

'Well, you're a boy aren't you?'

'Yes...'

'And you're a friend, so—'

'That's not the same thing!'

'Never mind, we're wasting time. We need to get in there.'

'We can't do that,' protested Kip.

'Why not?'

'Because...because...' He had a flash of inspiration. 'Because Mr Lazarus can only send one person into each film.' He glared at the projectionist. 'That's right, isn't it?'

Mr Lazarus considered for a moment, missing the point entirely.

'No,' he said. 'Not at all. If you both stand on the platform and hold hands, there's no reason why you can't go in together. And if you're doing the same thing when the Retriever button is pressed, all three of you can come out again.'

Kip groaned. 'Couldn't you have lied?' he snapped.

'Oh sorry, did you *want* me to lie?' Mr Lazarus looked crestfallen.

'That's settled then,' said Beth. 'We're both going in.' She looked at Mr Lazarus. 'That's if this isn't some big joke you're playing on us.'

'How can it be a joke?' asked Mr Lazarus. 'We can all see Rose up there on the screen, can't we? How could anybody have faked that?'

Beth frowned. It was a good question.

'Well,' said Mr Lazarus. 'I suppose we'd better get on with it.' He got the holster off the workbench and helped Kip strap it around his waist. Then he pulled out the earpiece and popped it into Kip's ear. He looked apologetically at Beth. 'I'm afraid I only have one Communicator,' he said.

'Er... that's OK,' said Beth, mystified. 'I guess.' She thought for a moment. 'What tariff is that thing on?' she asked.

'It isn't on any tariff,' said Mr Lazarus. 'Calls are free.'

'Yeah? Wow, where can I get one?'

'Never mind that,' Kip told her. 'We need to concentrate. And we're wasting time. We have to go after Rose.'

'Absolutely,' said Mr Lazarus, lifting a gloved hand to point at the ceiling. 'Time is of the essence.' He looked through the hatch at the screen. Rose's boat was just about to come ashore on a deserted stretch of beach. 'If we can get you in right beside her, you may be able to grab her and come straight back with

113

her. But, of course, what we can never allow for in these films are the edits.'

'What do you mean?' asked Beth.

'A film jumps along in time because of all the edits,' said Mr Lazarus. 'Rose can be in one place one moment and the very next, she could be ten miles away in a different location entirely. But when you're in the film, everything runs in real time, so it's possible, you might have a little catching up to do.'

'Oh, that's great,' said Kip. 'You never mentioned this before.'

'I didn't think I needed to. But think of all the cuts and dissolves and flashbacks there are in a modern film. You'd go crazy trying to deal with that! The Lazarus Enigma makes everything run just as it does in real life. But if you're unlucky and come in just as a cut takes place, your quarry could be a hundred miles away, two years later.'

'That would be a disaster,' said Kip.

'Hopefully it won't come to that. Anyway, enough talk. We'd better stop wasting time and get you onto Terror Island.' Mr Lazarus reached in his pocket and pulled out the Retriever.

'What's that thing?' asked Beth.

'The piece of equipment that will bring you back safe and sound,' said Mr Lazarus. 'But I must warn you. When the button is pressed, you must all be hanging tightly onto each other. If one person breaks contact, they'll be left behind.' He handed the device to Kip, who slung it around his neck and slipped it safely beneath his T-shirt.

'OK, let's do this,' he said. He looked at Beth. 'It's not too late to change your mind,' he told her.

'No way,' said Beth. 'I'm going with you. What kind of a girlfriend would I be if I left you to it?'

'There you go again,' said Kip. 'Girlfriend.'

'It's just an expression,' Beth assured him.

'Very well,' said Mr Lazarus. 'We're all ready. Step up onto the platform.'

Kip climbed on and Beth came to stand beside him. They found that standing face to face, they could just about manage it. Mr Lazarus made a final check on the equipment. 'Hold on tight to each other,' he warned them and they held hands. 'Here we go,' he said; and he put a foot onto the side of the platform. 'Good luck,' he added and pushed it forward into the light.

'Will it hurt?' asked Beth anxiously.

'Not really,' said Kip. 'It just feels a little weir—'

And then the light was blazing in his eyes and he realised he had no need to tell her what it felt like because that freaky melting feeling was coming over him again and he was falling, falling into a blinding white light.

CHAPTER THIRTEEN

THE ISLAND

Kip's feet thudded onto sand and he stood for a moment, letting his breathing settle back to normal. He could still feel other hands clutched in both of his and when he opened his eyes, there was Beth. She was staring around as though she could hardly believe what had happened.

'Oh my God!' whispered Beth. 'We're here. We're really here!'

And it *was* amazing. Even in the midst of all his worries about Rose, Kip had to take a moment to just marvel at his surroundings, which were perfect in every detail. He was standing on a long stretch of beach. To his left, the ocean rushed back and forth beneath the lurid red glow of the dying sun. Several hundred yards to his right, a stretch of dense jungle waited, the palm leaves stirring restlessly in the wind. Above them, the tropical sky was fading to grey, and he could already see the light of millions of stars and the cold orb of a full moon. And it wasn't just the look of the place. He could smell the salty tang of sea air. He could feel the grains of sand settling beneath his feet. The island was as real as any place he had ever visited.

Then Beth said, 'You can let go of my hands now.'

'Huh?' He looked at her and realised he had been squeezing her hands in his. 'Sorry.' He let go and turned to look around. There was the lifeboat already beached on the sand, completely empty – and there was a line of freshly made footprints, leading up the beach and away into the jungle.

'Oh no,' said Kip. 'She's already gone.'

'Must have been an edit,' suggested Beth. 'I guess we'd better follow the footprints. Hopefully they're not too far ahead.'

Kip stared into the dense jungle that lay ahead of them. He didn't much fancy the idea of wandering in there, but what other choice did he have?

Just then his mobile phone trilled the *Star Wars* theme. Wondering why Mr Lazarus was calling him on his regular phone, he snatched it from his pocket and lifted it to his ear, without thinking to look at the display.

'Why are you phoning me like this?' he asked.

'I was just checking you're all right,' said Dad's voice, sounding rather put out. Kip nearly fell down with shock. It hadn't occurred to him that other people would be able to contact him here.

'Oh er...Hi, Dad!' he stammered, aware of the horrified reaction from Beth. 'I was just er... surprised to hear from you so soon. How...how's Grannie?'

117

'She's fine,' said Dad. 'They've taken her into surgery, so I'll have to stay here till she comes out and they've got her settled. I've texted your mum but there's been no reply yet. How have you and Rose been getting along?'

'Rose? Oh...great! Yeah, she's great, Dad. But she's gone...'

'Gone? Gone where?'

'Gone...to the loo! Yes, I'm just waiting for her. Outside. Obviously, I can't go into the ladies, can I? So I'm just waiting by the door. You know, watching her like a hawk. Like you told me to. So...you... won't be able to talk to her right now.'

'Well, she won't be long, will she?'

'Er...I don't know. Depends whether she's doing a wee or a poo.'

'Thanks for the information! Well, I'll hang on for a while, just in case. I wanted to—' He broke off. 'Is it my imagination, or...can I hear the sea?'

'Umm? Oh, it's just...the...sound of the film from the auditorium,' said Kip hopelessly. 'Yes. The first bit is set at sea...I think.' He was aware of Beth staring at him, her mouth open.

'Kip, you're not in watching the film are you?'

'Of course not.' Kip laughed nervously. 'You know Rose, she'd never watch something like that.' He began to walk up the beach towards the jungle and Beth trailed after him. 'Ah, Rose is coming out now,' he said. 'Hi, Rose, you OK? We'll just head back to the ticket office now.' As they moved away from the water's edge, so the volume decreased. He stepped onto the jungle footpath and started walking briskly along it. Beth followed.

'So how's *Terror Island*?'

'Huh?' For a moment, Kip had the impression that Dad could somehow *see* where he was. Then he realised, he was only talking about the film. 'Oh... right! We've had a great first night. Packed out, very nearly a full house.'

'That's excellent news,' said Dad. 'I was worried takings were going to drop.'

'I told you it would do well,' said Kip. This felt weird. He was walking along a jungle trail, pushing his way through overhanging leaves and vines, and he was making small talk with his dad. Meanwhile, Rose was getting further and further away. 'Look, Dad, I really need to get on,' he said.

'Get on with what?'

'Er... somebody spilled popcorn in the foyer. I need to tidy it up.'

'All right. Just stick Rose on for a moment, OK?

'Er... right.' Kip looked over his shoulder at Beth and beckoned to her to catch up with him. 'OK, Dad, I'm putting Rose on now,' he announced. He held the phone out to Beth. She was shaking her head and making gestures with her hands that said, *No way!* Kip covered the phone with his hand for a moment, still staring intently at Beth. 'You've got to,' he whispered. Then he raised his voice slightly. 'Rose,' he said, 'Dad just wants a quick word with you.' He thrust the phone into Beth's hand. She lifted the handset to her ear as though it was a bomb that might go off at any moment. Kip heard a tiny insect-like voice as Dad asked a question.

Beth looked like she was walking on broken glass. When she spoke it was in a squeaky little voice that sounded, Kip thought, not so much like Rose but a constipated fairy.

'I'm fine, Daddy.' she squeaked. 'No, we weren't watching the film. I *hate* scary films.'

Dad's voice said something else.

'Oh yes, we're having a lovely time. I've been doing some colouring in. What do you mean, I sound different? I'm not different. Well, I'm not. No, I'm just the same as ever. Honestly.' A pause. 'Oh, all right then. Kip? Daddy wants to speak to you.' Beth thrust the handset back at Kip, looking daggers at him. He lifted it to his ear.

'Er . . . yes, Dad?'

'What's wrong with Rose?'

Kip swallowed.

'Nothing. She's fine.'

'She sounds *funny.*'

'Do you think so? Well, I'm not laughing. She's making me miss the film.'

'Yeah, don't start on about that. Anyway, I should be back around ten-thirty for the end of the movie.'

'That's fine, Dad,' said Kip. 'You take as long as you need.'

Just then the Communicator on his hip began to flash.

'Look, Dad, I've got to go. Somebody's come out for more popcorn.'

'OK. Catch you later.'

Kip rang off on the mobile and pressed the button on the Communicator.

'How are things progressing?' asked Mr Lazarus in his earpiece.

'Not great. I just had a phone call from Dad in Blackburn. I answered it without even thinking.'

'Oh dear. Do you think he suspected anything?'

'I just about got away with it . . . But never mind about that! We missed Rose on the beach. She's already left. Now we're walking along some kind of trail. Can you see us?'

'No. I'm further on into the film, watching Rose and the others. They're on the same trail I think, but further along it. I did warn you about the editing. The film must have jumped to a new scene just as you were touching down.'

'Well, what should we do?'

'Keep moving. If you step up the pace, hopefully you'll catch up with her before too long. Rose is with a blonde woman, who seems to be looking after her.'

'That'll be Kara Neetly, I suppose. OK, you'd better ring off. Call me if anything comes up.'

'I will. Good luck.' The Communicator went dead. Kip glanced at Beth. 'Bit creepy in here,' he observed, but she didn't reply. The trail was getting narrower and the jungle seemed to crowd in around them. There were sounds here, the rhythmic chirruping of insects, and a kind of hypnotic croaking sound.

'What's that noise?' asked Kip nervously.

'Tree frogs, I think,' said Beth. 'You get them in jungles.' She watched a lot of nature documentaries and prided herself on knowing about this kind of stuff. She was looking around, her expression one of delight. 'This is amazing,' she said. 'I always wanted to go into a jungle. What country do you think we're in?'

Kip didn't have the first idea. He was leading the way, peering along the narrow track, which twisted and turned through the thick ranks of vegetation. It was almost unbearably hot in here, a sweltering humid fug that made trickles of sweat run down his spine. It was also, despite the full moon, a lot darker than it had been on the beach. He tried not to think about how Rose must have felt being made to walk along here. He wondered how far ahead she was and hoped that he'd catch up with her before much longer.

Rose was hot and scared and fed up with trudging along the dark jungle trail. The sun had now slipped below the horizon and the light was fading fast. She was beginning to realise that this wasn't some kind of dream she was having. It all felt far too real for that. She clutched Tamara's hand tightly and looked around apprehensively. She wasn't sure how long they had been walking like this. All she knew was she wanted to be home in her own room, with her dolls and her cuddly toys. She looked up at Tamara and said, 'How much further?'

Tamara looked down and Rose could see that her pretty face was streaked with grime and sweat.

'I don't know, honey,' she said. 'We've just got to keep going.'

'What I wouldn't give for a flashlight,' muttered Captain Holder.

'Good job I grabbed one just before the ship went down,' said Jade. She reached into her pack and pulled out a heavy torch, which she handed to him. He looked at her with new respect in his eyes.

'How come you didn't mention this earlier?' he asked her.

'I was saving the batteries,' she told him.

He smiled, turned back and switched on the torch, directing a powerful beam of light along the trail. They started walking again.

'I don't like it here,' said Rose. 'There'll be bugs.'

'Ah, don't worry about them,' said Tad. 'The snakes will eat all the bugs.'

Tamara fixed him with a look.

'Now is probably not the time to be cracking jokes,' she said.

'Oh, excuse me all over the place,' said Tad. 'And besides, I wasn't joking. I'm simply stating a fact. A tropical rainforest like this is sure to have a high number of snakes. Big ones, I should think.'

'Will you shut up?' snapped Jade.

Tad looked crestfallen.

'I was only saying,' he muttered.

'Well, don't,' said Rose.

A few moments later, Captain Holder, who was walking at the head of the column, slowed a little and looked back over his shoulder.

'There's a building up ahead of us,' he announced.

'What kind of building?' asked Tamara.

'Hard to say. There's no lights or anything, place looks deserted.'

Now the trail opened out in to a clearing and the column of people was able to spread out a little. Rose could see the building that Captain Holder had mentioned; a modern-looking, three-storey structure that seemed strangely out of place in this primitive setting. It was encircled by a high chain-link fence topped by razor wire; and at intervals along its length were huge signs showing yellow lightning bolts, a sure indication that at one time the fence must have been electrified. But they could see that the huge set of metal gates set in the centre of the fence had been smashed open, as if by incredible force.

They walked closer, staring up at the shattered gates.

'What do you suppose happened here?' murmured Tad.

'Looks like something very powerful came through those gates,' said Captain Holder. 'A truck maybe.'

'But it's electrified,' said Jade.

'I'd say it was once upon a time,' admitted Captain Holder. 'But I reckon somebody switched off the juice.'

'How do you know?' asked Tad.

'I don't for sure, but if anybody feels like grabbing hold of the wire to test it, be my guest.' Nobody took him up on his offer. They walked in through the open gates and stood looking at the front entrance of the building. Above the door, a paint-blistered sign swung from a rusted-iron bracket. It was just possible to make out the words US MILITARY in faded yellow letters.

'Must be some kind of research centre,' said Tad. 'Hey, maybe there's a phone or a radio inside. We could call for help.'

'I wouldn't count on it, so I wouldn't,' said Sam, grimly. 'Place looks like it's been empty for years, so it does.'

A heavy wooden door barred the way. Captain Holder walked up to it and tested it with one powerful hand. There was a bit of give in it. He glanced round and saw a length of iron bar lying on the ground a short distance away. He fetched it and, handing the torch to Tad, he jammed the pipe into the door and began to exert all his strength to try and prise it open.

'I think this is called breaking and entering,' observed Tad.

'So sue me,' grunted Captain Holder through gritted teeth. The door opened surprisingly easily, making a scraping sound as it did so. Now they could all see that it had been half off its hinges and bore the evidence of having been forced open some time back. Somebody had simply closed it again.

Captain Holder dropped the metal bar, took back the torch and examined the inside of the door. 'That's odd,' he said. He indicated a huge metal bolt that nobody had bothered to use. 'If somebody had slid that across, I'd never have got it open.'

'I guess that means that there can't be anybody in here,' observed Tamara.

'But the door was closed,' reasoned Tad.

'Maybe from the outside?' suggested Jade.

'Unless there's somebody inside but they're too stupid to know how to use a bolt,' said Tad.

Jade laughed. 'Who could be that dumb?'

'Number Tails,' said Rose, remembering the creatures she had seen in the trailer, and everybody looked at her.

'What's that, honey?' asked Tamara.

'Number Tails,' said Rose. 'You know, like big monkey men?'

'What is she on about?' muttered Tad.

Captain Holder directed the beam of the torch into the building, revealing a scene of complete devastation. Everything was wrecked beyond repair. The floors were littered with piles of debris and a sparkling layer of broken glass. A wheelchair lay on its side, one wheel twisted and crumpled. A couple of ancient-looking computers lay in a corner, the screens smashed, the plastic casing shattered.

'What happened here?' asked Tamara.

'It was Number Tails,' said Rose. 'They look like big monkeys but they're scary like monsters.' Everybody looked at her again.

'*Monsters*?' cried Sam. 'Why do you keep saying that?'

'I saw the rotten trailer,' said Rose.

'The trailer?' muttered Tamara. 'You mentioned that before. What trailer?'

'The rotten trailer for the rotten film!'

Her companions exchanged puzzled glances.

'What's she talking about?' muttered Captain Holder.

'She seems to think we're in some kind of movie,' said Tamara.

'Interesting,' said Tad. 'That sounds like a form of dementia. Unusual in one so young.' Everyone ignored him.

'We *are* in a movie,' insisted Rose. 'Only, I'm not supposed to be in it. Just you lot. I don't know how I ended up here, but I did. And I know this is where the monster-men are. The Number Tails. I saw them chasing people.'

'Hey, quit that, kid,' said Tad. 'You're beginning to freak me out.'

'That makes two of us,' said Captain Holder. 'Come on, let's check inside. Everybody stay together.'

He started forward into the room, broken glass crunching beneath his boots.

'Think there's anybody else in here?' murmured Jade.

Tad shook his head.

'I'd say that's highly unlikely. There's no signs of life whatsoever.'

Just then, they heard a noise from somewhere up above them – a deep grunting sound.

'What the blue blazes was that?' asked Captain Holder.

CHAPTER FOURTEEN

LEG IT!

Kip and Beth came to a halt on the jungle trail. They stood there, looking fearfully around in the cold light of the full moon.

'What was that?' asked Kip quietly. They had both heard it – the sound of vegetation stirring, as though something large and heavy was moving through it.

'Probably some kind of jungle animal,' said Beth.

'Such as?' asked Kip.

'Er... well, it depends which country the island's in. It's a rainforest, so it could be a tapir, or a jaguar...'

'Or a sabre-toothed tiger,' said Kip. 'Remember, they were in the trailer?'

'Oh, but the creatures in this film are just CGI,' said Beth, 'computer animation. They couldn't be like... *real.*' She looked at Kip. 'Could they?'

Kip's grim expression must have said everything.

'But, that's mental,' said Beth.

Now there was another sound – a deep rumbling growl that seemed to shake the ground beneath them.

'That doesn't sound like anything I've heard on the Discovery channel,' admitted Beth. 'Maybe it's a—'

She broke off. They could hear something crashing along the trail behind them. They turned to look.

A long way back along the trail, a sabre-toothed tiger was coming after them – a lithe, tawny-coloured creature with powerful legs and jaws that looked like they could bite through steel cables. Even at this distance, they could see the long curved teeth that gave the beast its name glittering dangerously in the moonlight.

'Oh my God!' whispered Beth. 'I think that's supposed to be chasing the actors, like we saw in the trailer. Only...'

'Only we're in the way,' said Kip grimly.

'What do we do?'

'RUN!' yelled Kip, and he took off, as fast as his legs would carry him. Beth needed no second bidding. They raced along the narrow track, blundering through overhanging vegetation. Kip's heart was hammering in his chest and he felt a cold sweat of fear breaking out all over him.

'Press the button!' he heard Beth gasp.

'No way!' he said. 'We're not going back without Rose! If we bale out now, we can't save her. She'll be stuck in this film for ever.'

'Yeah, but listen...' Beth blundered into a bush and let out a string of colourful swear words. 'Being eaten alive won't help the situation!'

Kip was going to shout back an answer but at that moment, he slammed headlong into somebody who had just stepped out of the bushes to his right. It was like running in to a brick wall. A jolt of pure terror pulsed through him. A huge, muscular figure was towering over him and a hideous ape-like face stared blankly down into his eyes.

Kip just had time to think that this wasn't very promising and then a huge pair of hands clamped themselves around his throat. He was being lifted from the ground, his legs kicking frantically. He had a grandstand view of a prominent forehead and a mouth full of misshapen yellow teeth. His nostrils filled with the smell of intense body odour. He reacted instinctively, brought his feet up, planted them against the creature's chest and pushed with all his strength. In an instant, he tore free of the powerful grasp, but as he fell backwards he was aware of something around his neck that threatened to choke him. Almost instantly, the resistance was gone and he was falling backwards into Beth. Both of them collapsed on the ground.

'What is it?' gasped Kip.

'It's a Neanderthal,' said Beth's voice right beside his ear. 'A caveman.'

'But—'

'Push the bloody button!' yelled Beth.

Kip lifted a hand instinctively to grab the Retriever – and then realised it was no longer there. He looked up in mute horror as he saw that the Neanderthal had it. It was dangling by a length of chain from one of his huge hands, the crystal glinting like a jewel in the moonlight.

'Oh hell,' said Kip. A roar from just behind them, they snapped their gazes around to see that the sabre-toothed tiger was almost upon them – but just at that moment, an ear-shattering roar from the Neanderthal stopped the creature in its tracks. It turned aside and disappeared into the undergrowth.

Kip and Beth turned back, not sure whether to be grateful or terrified. The Neanderthal stood over them, staring defiantly about and grunting loudly as though challenging the sabre tooth to come back out and take him on. Then he seemed to notice the Retriever dangling from his fist. He stared at it and gave a grunt of surprise and cradled it in his other hand. As he did so, one huge thumbnail caught the metal cover and flipped it open, revealing the button with its pulsing red light.

'Don't touch that,' whimpered Kip. 'Please.'

The Neanderthal ignored him. His huge thumb pressed the EXIT button and then the creature's whole body seemed to shimmer and dissolve, right in front of Kip's astonished eyes. Quite suddenly, he was gone.

'Where the heck did he go?' gasped Beth.

Kip had a pretty good idea but didn't feel that now was the time to discuss it in any detail. He was horribly aware that the tiger was still out there somewhere, maybe observing them from the cover of the undergrowth. As if to enforce the point, there was a low rumbling growl from somewhere behind him and a sudden stirring in the bushes. He struggled back to his feet.

'Come on,' he said. He grabbed Beth's hand and they carried on running, the two of them blind to anything but the desperate need to escape.

Mr Lazarus was peering through the hatch at the cinema screen. He could see that Rose and her companions were moving cautiously through the dark building, guiding their way with a brilliant torch beam. He was just thinking of phoning Kip to advise him of this, when he heard the familiar whooshing sound that told him somebody was about to emerge from the film. Clearly Kip and Beth had run into trouble of some kind and had decided to make their escape. But they hadn't got Rose because she was still up there on the screen.

Mr Lazarus sighed. Now he would have to send them in again, but the problem was they were running out of time, the film was already at the halfway point. The projection room filled with an intense white light and something materialised on the wooden platform, which slid smoothly forward to the end of its track. Mr Lazarus stared in dismay at the creature that was sitting cross-legged on the platform. It certainly wasn't Kip, or anyone else he recognised.

The Neanderthal looked understandably baffled. He sat there, staring blankly around, his limited brain trying to work out what had happened to him. His long greasy hair framed a face that looked brutish and terrifying. His lower jaw seemed to extend further than his upper one and a series of broken yellow teeth stuck out from his mouth. He smelled even worse than he looked, like something that had been left lying in stagnant water for a very long time. The creature seemed to become aware of Mr Lazarus's presence. He made a threatening growl deep in his throat and began to clamber to his feet.

Mr Lazarus told himself not to panic. The obvious thing to do would be to push the platform straight back into the light, but to do this now would place the Neanderthal in the building where Rose and the others were currently searching through the rooms. The last thing Rose needed was this terrifying creature landing right beside her; and besides, it was necessary to get the Receiver out of the

Neanderthal's grasp before he did anything else. A creature so powerful could easily crush the delicate contraption and then there would be no way for Kip and the others to get out.

What to do? What to do?

Mr Lazarus had an idea. He reached a hand out to the sound system, which he used to play music in the intervals, knowing that a CD of Italian opera was already lined up ready to go. He punched the PLAY button and cranked up the volume. He realised that the music would intrude on the film but for the moment, there was nothing he could do about that. The sound of Pavarotti singing *Nessun Dorma* filled the room and the Neanderthal froze in his tracks, staring around, trying to identify the source of the sound. For the moment he had forgotten all about Mr Lazarus. His mouth opened and he gave a kind of sigh.

'Ah, so you like opera, do you?' murmured Mr Lazarus. 'Good.'

He kept the music playing, telling himself that he had only one chance to get this right. It was an idea born out of desperation and he wouldn't normally have tried something like this for a million pounds...but he really couldn't think of anything else to do. He reached out a hand to the projector and stopped the film.

One moment Kip was running for his life, as once again the tiger closed in on him and Beth. The next he was frozen, still in a running position, poised on his left leg. It was an alarming feeling. He wanted to turn his head to see how Beth was doing, but he could not move a muscle. And then, suddenly, horribly, he was running backwards at high speed, zooming back along the jungle trail. When he did manage to glance behind him, he could see Beth, a look of astonishment on her face as she sped down the trail in reverse. Just behind her, the sabre-toothed tiger was running backwards too and because it was so much faster than its prey, the gap between them was lengthening by the moment. Each time Kip glanced back, the tiger was further and further away until it had actually vanished from sight down the trail.

Kip tried to think what could be happening but even his thoughts were going in reverse, a hideous jumble of confusion and it was the strangest, most unpleasant feeling he had ever had in his life. Luckily it didn't last long. Quite suddenly, he was slowing to a backwards walk and after a few moments, he came to an abrupt standstill. There was a brief pause and then he was walking forward once more, at a normal speed. Thankfully his thoughts came back to him and he could at least understand them. And then there was a sudden noise.

'What was that?' asked Kip quietly. They had both heard it – the sound of vegetation stirring as though something large and heavy was moving through it.

'Probably some kind of jungle animal,' said Beth.

'Such as?' asked Kip.

'Er...well, it depends which country the island's in. It's a rainforest, so it could be a tapir, or a jaguar...'

They stared at each other. They had just simult-aneously had the sensation of déjà vu – the feeling that they'd done and said this before – and what's more, not so very long ago.

'That's it,' said Kip. 'This isn't working out. I'm going to use the Retriever.'

'Good idea,' said Beth. 'Better make it snappy. If I remember correctly, there's something coming down the trail after us.'

'A sabre-toothed tiger!' said Kip, remembering.

'Oh God, hurry up!'

'Don't worry,' said Kip. 'We're out of here.' He reached instinctively to his chest. 'We'll get Mr Lazarus to sort something out and send us back in at a safer—' He broke off as a dull sense of shock ran through him. 'Oh no,' he said.

'What?' Beth glared at him. 'What's wrong?'

'The Retriever. I've lost it.'

'You can't have!' protested Beth.

'I have, though,' wailed Kip. 'I...I seem to

138

remember losing it before... There was somebody further along the trail and—'

A distant rumbling growl seemed to shake the ground beneath their feet. They looked at each other.

'Leg it!' yelled Kip and he didn't have to ask twice. Beth had remembered what came next. They both knew that they needed as much of a head start as they could get. They took off just as fast as their legs would carry them.

The Communicator started flashing. Kip pressed the button without even breaking stride.

'Mr Lazarus!' he yelled. 'I've lost the Retriever!'

'Yes, dear boy, I know,' said a voice in his ear. 'But please don't worry, it's back here with me.'

'But... how did that happen?'

'All I know is that a Neanderthal must have taken it from you... and I suppose that it must have happened somewhere between where you are now and the building where Rose is.'

'How do you know it was a Neanderthal?'

'Ah, that's a simple deduction. He's here with me too.'

For a moment Kip was speechless. 'Mr Lazarus, are you saying there's a Neanderthal in the Paramount?'

'Yes, I'm afraid so. Rather inconvenient actually. But don't worry, it's only a temporary arrangement. For the moment I'm distracting him with opera.'

Kip looked back at Beth.

'There's a Neanderthal in the Paramount!' he shouted. 'Mr Lazarus is playing him some opera.'

'Oh, that's nice,' yelled Beth. 'And has he made him a cup of tea and some cucumber sandwiches?'

Kip ignored that one. He lifted the Communicator again.

'Everything's going mental here,' shouted Kip. 'We've been running backwards.'

'Ah yes, that was me rewinding the film. Very unpredictable, I hate doing it but it was the only thing I could think of.'

'Well, thank God you did. We were about to be eaten by a sabre-toothed tiger!'

'Really? That sounds most unpleasant. Listen, you are all out of breath. Can't you slow down a moment?'

'No we can't! It'll be coming after us again at any second and it's way faster than we are.'

Beth was glancing nervously over her shoulder down the trail. 'I think I see it coming,' she yelled. 'Kip, we've got to do something!'

'Kip, listen to me!' Mr Lazarus had an urgent tone to his voice. 'I don't know how long I can keep the caveman's attention. He looks dangerous.'

'Not as dangerous as this tiger. Can't you see it?'

'I can't see you, remember. I'm further on in the film, watching Rose and her companions. I'm assuming you're still back somewhere on the trail?'

'Yes we are!'

'Well, I need to send this caveman back into the film. Now, don't panic. I'm going to fast-forward you for a moment.'

'What?' Kip was horrified. 'Don't do that. The tiger will catch up with us even quicker!'

'It'll be all right, trust me. I can't risk putting the caveman into the building where Rose is. Or at least where she *will* be in a few moments, if you catch my drift. I'm going to try and time it so he comes back into events after they've gone inside.'

'Oh, but you're perfectly happy to just dump him on us!'

'There's a long panning shot of the jungle just before Rose and her companions reach the building, I'm going to try and drop him in there. That should give her time to get back inside.'

'I don't understand...'

'Don't worry. You just need to be aware that the caveman will be arriving somewhere near the top of the trail and whatever you do, you mustn't run into him. Keep the Communicator on and I'll warn you when he's coming.'

'Wait, wait, what about the Retriever?'

'Ah yes. Well, I'll have to send that in later, to a safe place. Assuming I can get it away from the Neanderthal; he seems rather attached to it.'

'He seems *what*?'

'Never mind, I'll tell you where it's going to be

141

once I've sent it in. Now, what is it they used to say on all the best fairground rides? Oh yes. Scream if you want to go faster!'

'But wait, we—'

'No time, Kip. I'm hitting the button now!'

Kip's mouth was open to ask another question but then, with a horrible lurching sensation deep in the pit of his stomach, he found himself whizzing along the jungle trail at an insane speed, trying desperately to avoid crashing into bushes and overhanging foliage. He risked glancing back once to see that Beth was right behind him, her astonished expression telling him that she was feeling just as confused as he was. And now, right on cue, the tiger appeared on the trail behind them, closing the space at incredible speed.

'Don't worry!' he shrieked and his speeded-up voice made him sound like somebody who had been inhaling helium from a party balloon. 'I think Mr Lazarus knows what he's doing!'

'God I hope so,' shrieked Beth, glancing back down the trail at the huge pair of slavering jaws that were gaining on her by the second.

Mr Lazarus hoped he was doing the right thing. It was risky, but for the life of him he couldn't think of anything else that might work. He still had his Communicator pressed to one ear, from which issued the sounds of frantic, speeded-up motion, feet crashing through dense undergrowth and the occasional high-pitched roar. The caveman was now swaying from side to side on the wooden platform, seemingly entranced by the music, which was still blasting from the speakers. The Retriever dangled by its chain from one of his hands, totally forgotten.

Mr Lazarus edged carefully closer and reached out his free hand for it. At the last moment, the caveman seemed to remember that he was not alone. His ugly face contorted into an expression of rage and his eyes blazed with feral anger.

'Now, now, don't be a difficult Neanderthal!' Mr Lazarus told him. 'I'm going to send you on a little trip. I'm sure you'd like that, wouldn't you?'

Mr Lazarus glanced through the hatch at the screen, waiting for the right moment. Then he saw the start of the long panning shot. Perfect.

'Time to go!' he yelled.

The Neanderthal grunted and gave him a questioning look.

In the same instant Mr Lazarus grabbed the Retriever, wrenched it out of the Nenaderthal's grasp and placed one foot against the edge of the platform. Then he pushed with all his strength, sending it gliding back into the light.

'One large angry Neanderthal coming in!' he yelled.

The caveman gave a despairing bellow of baffled rage and then his huge body began to shimmer and dissolve. An instant later, he was gone.

Kip heard Mr Lazarus's voice shouting its warning and he tried to be on his guard – but it wasn't easy racing through the jungle at a hundred miles an hour with a hungry tiger in hot pursuit.

For the moment nothing happened, but he reminded himself that Mr Lazarus was further on in the film. The Neanderthal would most likely appear somewhere along the track. He glanced briefly back and there was the tiger, gaining on him and Beth by the second, his mouth open in a ferocious snarl and those hideous, oversized teeth glittering in the moonlight.

Luckily Kip's thoughts seemed as speeded up as his actions and, when he caught a glimpse of a heavy fallen branch at the side of the track, he managed to snatch it up without slowing his pace. He ran grimly on, steeling himself, and then he saw something materialising on the track ahead of him: a great big ugly creature with a hideous face. At the same instant there was that odd feeling of déjà vu again, but there was no time to think about that, because he knew he had to get past the Neanderthal – at all costs.

As he ran, he lifted the tree branch in both hands. The Neanderthal was moving relatively

144

slowly compared to Kip and he began to turn to face the oncoming runners, an expression of dull surprise on his brutish features. As the gap closed between them, Kip swung the branch at the Neanderthal's head and it connected with a force that would have felled an ordinary person. As it was, the creature gave a grunt of surprise and reeled back a couple of steps, enough to allow the two frantic runners to whiz by him. He recovered himself in an instant and stumbled back to the track with a bellow of rage, only to find himself stepping right into the path of a very hungry tiger.

Behind him Kip heard a stomach-churning shriek and then a heavy impact as the Neanderthal was knocked backwards into the undergrowth. Then there was what sounded like a pitched battle between tiger and Neanderthal. Kip kept right on running, not daring to look back.

For a few minutes, Kip and Beth continued to race along but then with another lurch they slowed back to normal speed. They were still running, but compared to their previous speed, it seemed as if they were just creeping along.

A few moments later, the jungle trail began to widen out and they were able to slow to a trot and then to a walk, glancing back as they did so to ensure that nothing was close enough to give them any trouble. At last they dared to come to a halt. They stood there, panting as they tried to get their breathing back to normal.

Beth was the first to speak.

'That was . . . mental,' she said.

Kip nodded, but for the moment, he couldn't find words.

'What was that about a Neanderthal at the Paramount?' gasped Beth.

'Oh no, he's back in the film now,' Kip assured her. 'That was the one I . . . clouted with the stick.' He pointed back down the trail. 'The one who just ended up as dinner for a sabre-toothed tiger.' He shook his head. 'I can't help feeling a bit bad about that. He stepped right out in front of it.'

'Never mind about him,' snapped Beth. 'Just be grateful it wasn't us. Now, tell me how we're going to get home without the Retriever.'

'We can't.'

'Oh perfect. So that means we're stuck here?'

'No, don't worry, Mr Lazarus is going to send the Retriever back into the film, once he finds somewhere safe to leave it.'

'Oh really?' Beth seemed amused by this idea. 'And where would that be exactly?' It was clear from the tone of her voice that she was starting to get very annoyed.

'Maybe there,' said Kip pointing. Up ahead of them, stark and grey in the moonlight, stood a dilapidated, three-storey building. 'This must be the place Mr Lazarus mentioned,' he added, starting forward.

'It looks pretty scary,' said Beth. 'There could be all kinds of things hanging around in the shadows.'

'Can't help that,' Kip told her. 'I'm pretty sure that's where Rose is, so that's where we're going.'

Beth sighed. 'It just keeps getting better,' she said.

'Look, I didn't want you to come here in the first place,' Kip told her. 'You insisted on tagging along.'

'Yes, but I didn't know you were going to lose the Retriever, did I?'

'I didn't *lose* it. It was taken from me; there's a difference.'

'You should have been more careful.'

'Beth, a dirty great Neanderthal pulled it from around my neck. What was I supposed to do, ask him for it back?'

'Well no, obviously, but couldn't you have grabbed it as we ran past?'

'How could I? He didn't have it any more. It's back with Mr Lazarus at the Paramount.'

'This is so confusing,' said Beth.

'Well there's no point in arguing about it now,' said Kip. 'Come on, we need to check this place out.'

They approached the shattered metal gates.

'What do you make of it?' asked Kip.

Beth frowned. 'In films like this, they usually turn

147

out to be top-secret research centres run by the US military,' she said. She noticed the sign above the open door and pointed to it. 'Bingo.'

'Looks like the fence used to be electrified,' observed Kip. 'But that gate's been hit by something big and powerful.'

'Probably a dinosaur,' said Beth. 'Like in *Jurassic Park*.'

'Wrong era,' said Kip. 'You don't get Neanderthals and dinosaurs around at the same time.'

'Tell that to the people who made *One Million Years BC*,' said Beth. 'If you're expecting this film to be historically accurate, think again.'

They went in through the smashed gates and approached the building, gazing apprehensively up at the barred windows and sheer walls.

'You really think we should go in there?' muttered Beth.

'We have to. I'm sure Rose is in there.'

Beth was about to reply but was interrupted by an all too familiar roar that made them both jump. They looked back the way they had come and saw the tiger emerging at the top of the jungle trail, its jaws dripping with fresh blood.

'Oh perfect,' said Kip. 'Let's get inside.'

They ran towards the open doorway at the front of the building and stepped into the gloom of what had once been the building's foyer. Turning back, they grabbed the door and swung it shut. It was hanging from one hinge and needed quite a bit of effort to get it closed, the grinding sound of wood on tiled floor echoing around the big empty room. Kip noticed a strong metal bolt and slammed it home, just a few moments before a mighty impact pounded against the wood, making the whole door shudder in its frame.

Kip looked frantically about, realising that the door wouldn't hold such a powerful creature back for very long. He noticed a rusty fridge standing off in one corner and shouted to Beth to help him with it. They ran to it and struggled to drag it across the littered floor to the doorway. They got it in position just in time and shoved it against the shuddering wood.

Kip and Beth backed away, staring fearfully at the door. Already the pounding was causing the ancient wood to shudder. Beth pointed at the barred windows. 'Hopefully it can't get through those,' she said. 'But I don't know how long that door's going to hold.'

'Hopefully long enough,' said Kip. 'Come on, let's find Rose.'

CHAPTER FIFTEEN
THE FACILITY

'What the hell just happened to us?' asked Captain Holder. It was a question that none of his companions had a ready answer for. To Rose, it had all been a bit of a blur. They'd entered the building and stood in the dark and creepy foyer, looking around. Then they'd heard a noise, a kind of snuffling, grunting sound. They'd started to search for the source of the sound but then, without any warning, they'd all been frozen in position for several moments, unable to move so much as a finger.

This was scary enough, but then something *really* weird had happened. They'd all walked rapidly backwards out of the building, retracing their steps until they were back in the jungle clearing where they'd first seen the building. There they'd stopped for a moment and Captain Holder had opened his mouth to ask what was going on . . . and then, totally against their will, they were moving forward again, this time at unbelievable speed. They'd raced in through the open doorway; they'd registered the strange sound and had conducted a frantic search through a whole series of creepy-looking rooms on the ground floor.

It was the kind of thing you really wanted to do as slowly and carefully as possible, but it had all been done at a flat-out sprint. They'd tried talking to each other and what had come out of their mouths had sounded like excited children babbling nonsense. Finally, they'd heard a noise in one of the rooms and had gone inside to investigate. Rose had noticed a sudden movement in one dark corner and she'd screamed, her voice sounding unbelievably shrill. This had spooked everyone and in a total panic, they'd all raced full pelt out of the room and up a staircase to the first floor.

Finally, unexpectedly, everything had slowed back to normal and here they stood, on a deserted landing, out of breath and completely baffled.

'That was . . . nuts,' said Tamara. 'I couldn't stop myself . . . from moving that way.' She looked down at Rose. 'Are you OK, honey?'

Rose nodded. But she didn't feel OK. She felt weird.

'I want to go home,' she said. She thought if she said it often enough, it might just happen.

'Well, whatever it was, it's stopped now,' said Jade.

'No kidding,' said Tad. 'Gee, I'm glad you're with us, Jade. Without your lightning-fast observations, we wouldn't know what's happening.'

Jade gave him a cold look.

'Tad, maybe if you stopped wisecracking all the time, we might be able to figure out what's happening here.' She looked around at the others. 'Where's Sam?' she asked.

Everyone reacted in total dismay. They had all thought the first mate was with them, but there was no sign of him.

'He was right behind me when we ran out of that room,' said Tad. 'The one where we heard the noises. The one where we saw something moving in the shadows. The one where the kid screamed.'

'You left him behind?' growled Captain Holder.

'I didn't *leave him*,' protested Tad. 'I mean, not on purpose. Like I said, he was right behind me. At least, I *thought* he was.'

There was a puzzled silence.

'I guess the Number Tails got him,' said Rose.

Everyone stared at her.

'What are you talking about?' snapped Captain Holder.

'That's how it works in movies,' explained Rose. 'If Kip was here, he'd be able to tell it better. He says it's one of the rules in scary films. The person with the smallest part always gets the chop first. And Sam hardly ever spoke. It makes sense he'd be first to go.'

'Stop talking like that,' snapped Captain Holder. 'Sam's my best friend.'

'You didn't say that when he sank your boat,' said Rose.

'Maybe not,' admitted Captain Holder, sheepishly. 'But he's worked for me for a long time. I'm going down to look for him. Who's coming with me?'

There was an uncomfortable silence. Nobody seemed to be able to look him in the eye.

'OK,' he said. 'If that's how you feel . . .' He started towards the stairs but stopped at the sound of a series of footsteps pounding in through the front entrance below. 'What the hell is that?' he whispered.

'It'll be the Number Tails,' Rose told him again. 'Come on, we need to hide.'

'But, what about Sam?'

'He'll be brown bread by now,' said Rose. 'That's what Kip always says. I think it means "dead". Him and Beth have this game where they watch a movie and they try to guess which order everybody gets to be brown-breaded. They're hardly ever wrong.'

'Who's Kip?' asked Tad irritably.

'My brother, and he's seen more scary films than anyone in the world,' said Rose. 'I wish he was here now, he'd know what to do.'

'You're a real little ray of sunshine,' said Tad. 'Anyone ever tell you that?'

'I'm just telling the truth,' said Rose. 'And if I was you, I'd stop saying nasty things. People who do that don't last very long in these films.'

Tad swallowed nervously and, for once, didn't seem to have a reply.

Now there were more noises from downstairs – a loud scraping and bumping as though something heavy was being dragged across the floor.

'We really should go down there and look for Sam,' muttered Captain Holder, but nobody made a move towards the staircase. He looked around at their grim, sweating faces. 'OK,' he said. 'I guess he'll just have to take his chances. Let's have a look around up here.' He led the way along the landing and the others followed him.

Kip and Beth crept along a corridor on the ground floor, peering cautiously through each open doorway they came to. It was almost completely dark, with only the occasional bit of moonlight pouring in to each room through a barred window.

'I wish we'd brought a torch with us,' said Beth quietly. They were both horribly aware of thumping, crashing noises coming from the direction of the main entrance.

Kip didn't say anything. He was too intent on finding Rose to think about much else. He peered cautiously through the doorway of the next room he came to. It appeared to be as wrecked as everywhere else and looked like it had been some kind of laboratory. He saw a stainless-steel operating table and a litter of lab equipment – broken test tubes, Bunsen burners and, against one wall, a whole row of refrigerators. He went in cautiously, aware of broken glass crunching beneath his feet. Beth followed close behind.

'She won't be in here,' said Beth.

'Don't be so sure,' warned Kip. 'There's plenty of places to hide in here.'

'Why would she be hiding?' asked Beth.

'How many reasons do you need?' said Kip. 'I feel like hiding myself.' In the silence they could hear crashing sounds coming from along the hall. The tiger was still trying to break down the door.

'Why doesn't it give up?' muttered Kip.

'I guess it's hungry,' said Beth.

'How can it be? It's just eaten a whole Neanderthal.'

'We don't know that it ate the whole thing,' argued Beth. 'Maybe it just nibbled on him. I reckon we'd be a bit more tender.'

'Will you stop talking about stuff like that?' protested Kip. 'I really don't want to think about being eaten right now.'

'Sorry,' said Beth. 'Look, maybe we should go up to the next floor.'

'Shush!' Kip thought he heard movement coming from a dark corner of the room. 'Rose, is that you?' he muttered. He took a step forward and his foot clunked against something. He stooped, groped around and his hands connected with something metal. He picked up a heavy machete. In the dim wash of moonlight, he could see that the blade was black with dried blood, but he hung onto it anyway, telling himself that at least it was some kind of a weapon. Again, he heard that sound – a rustling. 'Rose?' He moved closer to the dark corner.

'Don't bother,' said Beth, her voice filled with dread. 'It won't be her.'

'Quiet!' snapped Kip. 'We don't know that.'

'Sure we do,' Beth warned him. 'You've seen films like this. They always have things jumping out of the dark to scare you.'

'Pipe down will you? I can't hear myself think.'

Kip edged closer into the corner.

'Rose?' he whispered, and he thought he heard a low gasp coming from out of the darkness. It sounded like the kind of sound his sister might make if she was crying. 'Rose, don't be scared,' he whispered. 'It's me, Kip.'

He reached out a hand into the darkness and his fingers touched something soft and warm, but it didn't feel like a little girl. Suddenly, shockingly, something bit deep into the back of his hand, sending a jolt of pain flickering up his arm. He yelled and jumped back with a curse and then something powerful came flapping up out of the darkness at him, something big with leathery wings and wild eyes that seemed to shine in the darkness. He also got a flash of some razor-sharp teeth but then he was too busy trying to get away from the creature, which came swooping down at his head, its huge wings flapping madly, battering him like a flurry of punches. It was as big as an umbrella.

He remembered the machete in his hand and flailed wildly at the creature, which emitted an unearthly screech but kept right on coming.

'What is it?' he yelled as he stumbled around the room, trying to swat the thing away from him.

'A bat,' offered Beth helpfully, looking about for some kind of weapon. 'A vampire bat, I think.' She saw a broom standing against one wall and snatching it up, she ran forward and swung wildly at the creature, but her aim was bad and she only succeeded in swiping Kip across the back of the head.

'Ow! Do me a favour. Stop helping!' yelled Kip. He lashed out with the machete again and provoked another shriek from the bat. Warm, sticky fluid splashed down onto his face and the huge creature flapped up towards the ceiling, injured but far from dead.

'Oh, gross!' muttered Beth. 'Let's get out of here.'

They retreated towards the door and the bat came after them again, flapping and shrieking madly. Kip was the last out of the room. The bat made a determined swoop for him and he slammed the door shut. There was a heavy impact on the other side as the bat piled headfirst into it. There was the brief sound of beating wings and then all went quiet. Kip frowned, looking down at the back of his hand, which had two huge puncture marks in it.

'Nice,' he said. 'That thing was after my blood.'

'Told you not to go in there,' said Beth.

Kip looked at her. 'You got a better plan?' he muttered.

'Yes. I think we should head up to the next floor.' She glanced apprehensively down the corridor to the main doors, where the tiger was still doing its best to smash its way through.

'But there's loads more rooms down here,' argued Kip. 'Rose could be in any one of them. Supposing we go up there and she's down here and that tiger manages to batter through the door.'

'But I really think she'll be upstairs.'

'What makes you say that?'

'It seems more likely somehow.'

'But that's just a *guess!*' protested Kip. 'You really have no idea where she is. Just give me one good reason why you think she might be up there.'

At that moment, the Communicator started flashing. Kip pressed the button and a familiar voice spoke in his ear.

'Kip,' said Mr Lazarus. 'I just thought I'd let you know. Rose and her companions are up on the first floor.'

'Oh . . . er . . . right,' said Kip. He glanced sheepishly at Beth then looked away. 'We're on the ground floor right now,' he told Mr Lazarus. 'We'll get straight up there.' He began to lead the way back along the corridor and gestured to Beth to follow him.

'Told you,' said Beth. Kip ignored her.

'Listen,' said the voice in his ear. 'I'm going to send the Retriever up there. Rose and the others are in a room filled with incubators.'

'What are they?' asked Kip.

'Like big glass boxes; the things that premature babies are placed in. I have to act quickly before they leave the room. You'll need to go up there and find the room, it's to the left of the staircase. Remember, without the Retriever none of you can come back. I also thought I should warn you, the film has only got thirty minutes left to run.'

'OK. But look, if it gets really close, can't you rewind the film again, like you did before?'

'What would be the point of that? You won't get any closer to Rose. You have to make a real effort to catch up with her.'

'We're trying,' protested Kip.

'Try harder. I'm sending the Retriever in now.'

The earpiece went dead.

A particularly loud crash from the direction of the main door reminded Kip that they probably didn't have time to stand around and discuss this.

'Come on,' he said. 'The staircase is back in the foyer. Hopefully, we can—'

He stopped talking. A figure had just stepped out of a room up ahead and was walking away from them along the corridor. Even in the dim light they could see he was dressed in a yellow raincoat.

'Hey,' said Kip. 'I think that's one of the guys from the film.'

He started forward and Beth followed him.

'His name's Sam, I think,' she said.

'Yeah, that's right,' said Kip. 'Hey, Sam, wait up a minute!'

The man stopped walking. He turned slowly round to face Kip and Beth and they froze in their tracks. It wasn't Sam – not unless he had suddenly grown another foot in height, had thrown away his shoes and trousers and had developed a sloping forehead. What they were looking at was a Neanderthal, who for reasons best known to himself, had put on Sam's yellow raincoat. It was way too small for him and didn't even begin to cover his hairy chest. He stared at the newcomers and made a kind of snuffling, grunting sound. Kip noticed that he had something big in one hand – something he was chewing on.

'I wonder what happened to Sam,' he muttered.

'I think I know,' said Beth bleakly.

Then Kip realised just exactly what it was the Neanderthal was eating. It was a human arm. He was gnawing on it like it was the biggest chicken drumstick in the world.

'Ewww!' said Beth. 'Minging!'

The Neanderthal studied them both for a moment. Then he spat out a finger and dropped the arm on the floor. Clearly he thought he had just spotted something tastier.

'Oh hell,' murmured Kip. 'He's looking at us funny.'

'Well nobody's laughing,' said Beth. 'I didn't realise Neanderthals were cannibals.'

'They are in *this* film,' said Kip. 'That's all that matters.'

Now the Neanderthal was moving towards them, studying them intently. A low growl came from him and he licked his lips. Beth nudged Kip urgently.

'You'll have to do the business,' she said.

'The business?' Kip looked down at the machete in his hand and then shook his head. 'Oh, no way,' he whispered. 'I'm not doing that.'

The Neanderthal gave a horrible rasping chuckle. He was staring at Kip as though he was a Big Mac with legs. His eyes seemed to blaze with an unholy light.

'You'll *have* to,' said Beth.

'I'm not cutting somebody's head off!' hissed Kip. 'Not even somebody who's planning to eat me.' He thrust the machete at her. 'You do it!'

'I can't!' protested Beth. 'I . . . I'm practically a vegetarian. It . . . it's up to you, Kip. Rose is *your* sister.'

'What's that got to do with anything?'

The two of them were backing along the corridor now and the Neanderthal kept following them. A glow of moonlight from a skylight illuminated his face for a moment and they could see that his chin and chest were plastered with blood. They were now backing past the doorway from which the Neanderthal had emerged.

Kip decided to try something desperate. He pointed in through the open doorway. 'Oh, wow, look at that!' he yelled.

The Neanderthal turned to look into the room, his mouth hanging open. Kip slipped in behind him, lifted a leg and placed a boot against the caveman's backside. Then he pushed with all his strength. The Neanderthal lost his balance and was catapulted through the doorway, his arms flailing. There was a crash from within as he collided with something breakable. Then Kip grabbed the door and slammed it shut. He noticed there was a key in the lock and he turned it.

'RUN!' he yelled, and he and Beth sprinted along the corridor, back to the foyer. When they got there, they saw to their dismay that the heavy entrance door was beginning to splinter beneath the onslaught of the tiger's claws. It couldn't last much longer. Kip glanced up the staircase into total darkness.

'We can't go up there in the pitch black,' he said. 'We need some kind of light.' He indicated a row of metal lockers behind the reception desk. 'There have to be torches somewhere.'

'What makes you think that?' asked Beth.

'In films like this there are *always* torches,' he yelled. He threw open the nearest cupboard and set about rifling through the contents. Beth was standing there studying the rapidly disintegrating front door. 'Help me!' shouted Kip. She seemed to come out of a trance and sprang to the lockers, began throwing them open, one by one, pulling out the contents and scattering them on the floor, wincing at every blow against the entrance door. Now they could actually see moonlight filtering in through the places where the tiger's claws had shredded the wood.

'We need to get up those stairs,' said Beth.

'We can't go up in the dark,' insisted Kip. 'Anything could jump out at us. Keep looking.'

The sound of a door being smashed open made him look back down the corridor. He saw a shambling figure in a yellow raincoat come staggering through the doorway of the room into which he had been pushed. The Neanderthal stood for a moment as though uncertain of which way to go. Then he turned, spotted his prey and came striding towards them, his brutish face contorted with anger.

'Here comes laughing boy!' announced Kip.

Beth had found a metal locker against one wall.

'I think this could be a strong possibility,' she yelled.

'What makes you say that?' asked Kip.

'It's got the word *Torches* written on it.'

'Great,' said Kip.

'Only it's padlocked.'

'Not so great.' Kip hurried over to her and looked at the padlock, a chunky iron contraption. 'Why did they lock the bloody thing?' he asked the room in general. 'Didn't they realise people might be in a hurry?'

'Probably trying to create suspense,' suggested Beth.

'It's working,' said Kip.

There was another splintering sound and a great big paw tore its way clean through the entrance door.

'Hurry!' yelled Beth.

Kip lifted the machete, took aim and brought it down as hard as he could on the padlock. The rusted metal shattered beneath the impact and he was able to fling open the door. They stood staring, hardly believing their luck. There were half a dozen torches in the cupboard, and several packs of batteries.

'Yes!' said Kip. He dropped the machete, pulled out one of the torches and flicked the switch.

Nothing happened. 'No,' he said. Sweat was pouring down his face now and out of the corner of his eye, he was aware that the front door was virtually coming off its hinges. Through the gap he could see a pair of malignant yellow eyes staring in at him.

'Move it!' yelled Beth. She was jumping up and down on the spot in her torment. Kip grabbed another torch and threw it to her. Then he tossed her a pack of batteries. From the corner of his eye, he was horribly aware of the yellow-coated Neanderthal lurching towards him along the corridor. Kip struggled to rip open the cellophane wrapping on a pack of batteries, tearing at it with his teeth. It split across the middle, spilling batteries onto the floor. He swore, stooped and grabbed a couple of them. He twisted open the end of the torch and slammed the new batteries into it, his hands shaking. He twisted the cap back on the end of his torch and jumped upright with a yell of triumph.

'Right, let's get up those—'

He broke off as a pair of hairy hands clamped around his throat and lifted him clear off the ground. Kip could feel the incredible strength in those hands. They were squeezing the life out of him. He kicked and struggled and even reached up with the torch and slammed it down hard on the Neanderthal's head but it had no effect. A red heat filled his head and he could barely struggle any more.

Then there was a sharp hiss as something metallic sliced through the air. The Neanderthal's expression changed to one of surprise, his eyes bulging, his mouth hanging open. He froze in position for a moment, his arms still outstretched. Then his head tilted sideways. It kept tilting, moving past the point where any head should be able to tilt and then it slipped off his neck and fell. It went bouncing along the littered floor like an oddly-shaped football. A few moments later, the hands lost their power and released Kip. The body fell too, completely devoid of any life.

Kip looked down at it in amazement. Then he looked up again. Beth was standing there, a grim expression on her pretty face. She had the bloody machete in one hand.

'Somebody had to,' she whispered.

Kip stared at her. He had a sudden impulse to take her in his arms and kiss her, but realised that there probably wasn't time for that.

'Thanks,' he croaked. 'I owe you one.'

There was an almighty crash as the heavy refrigerator tipped forward and hit the ground. The two friends looked up in absolute terror and saw that the tiger was pushing through the shattered remains of the door.

Without another word, they turned and ran for the stairs, switching on their torches as they went.

CHAPTER SIXTEEN
COMINGS AND GOINGS

Captain Holder led the way into the large window-less room and the others followed him. They were all aware of noises coming from downstairs – loud thuds and crashes, shrieks and roaring sounds, but none of them were in a big hurry to go and see what was causing them. Captain Holder shone his torch around the interior, revealing rows and rows of oblong Perspex boxes.

'Fish tanks!' exclaimed Rose.

'No, honey,' said Tamara, gently. 'They're incubators. This must have been where they kept premature babies.'

'Funny-looking babies,' said Jade and the torchlight showed that one of the tanks was filled with large fleshy grey eggs. 'What kind of a bird lays eggs like that?' she muttered.

'I don't think they're bird eggs,' said Tad. 'I'd say they came from some kind of large serpent.' Everybody ignored him.

'They still look like fish tanks to me,' said Rose. She let go of Tamara's hand and moved along a line of transparent boxes, peering into each of them in turn. She saw one had a big hole punched in the side of it and was full of broken eggs, but all the others were empty...no, not *all* of them. As she peered in to the sixth box along, there was a sudden shimmering light within it and something seemed to materialise, right in front of her eyes. She found herself looking at a funny, glowing contraption on a length of chain. She frowned. She was sure it hadn't been there a moment ago. She noticed a little door on the front of the box, so she unlatched the cover, and reached in to take hold of the gadget. It was pulsing with a slow red light that seemed to be coming from beneath a metal cover. She was able to lift the cover up, revealing a black button with the word EXIT written on it. She lifted the thing closer and reached out a finger to press the button.

'Hey, hang on, kid, what have you got there?' asked Captain Holder, moving closer with the flashlight.

'I don't know,' said Rose. 'It just appeared in the fish tank. Like magic.'

'Interesting,' said Tad. 'Sounds like some kind of matter transfer.'

Everyone ignored him.

Captain Holder reached out and took the gadget from Rose's hand. He examined it in the torchlight.

'I've never seen anything like this before,' he said. 'I wonder what it does.'

'Better not mess with it,' warned Tad. 'Press that button and you could blow the whole place sky high.'

'Don't be ridiculous,' said Captain Holder. 'Why would there be something like that in here?'

'Anything's possible in this screwy place,' said Jade.

'But the button is marked EXIT,' said Captain Holder. 'Maybe it activates some kind of escape equipment – a way out of here.'

'Sounds reasonable,' Tamara agreed. 'It has to be worth a try.'

Captain Holder looked around at the others.

'What do you think?' he asked them.

'I say go for it,' said Jade.

'I'm not so sure,' said Tad.

'I'm with Jade on this one,' said Tamara.

'Whatever,' said Rose.

Captain Holder considered for a moment. In the silence there were more violent crashing sounds from downstairs.

'Well,' he murmured, 'here goes.' He pressed the button. There was a brief flash of light. His entire body seemed to shimmer for an instant and then quite suddenly, he disappeared. Unfortunately, he had taken the only source of light with him. The team found themselves plunged abruptly into almost total darkness.

'Where the hell did he go?' asked Jade.

'I told you it sounded like matter transfer,' said Tad huffily. 'How come nobody ever listens to me?'

'Well, he can't just have disappeared,' said Tamara. 'He must be around here somewhere.' She peered about in the gloom, trying to find her bearings. 'I can't see a thing.'

'There's no windows in here,' complained Jade. 'We need to get out and find a bit of moonlight.'

'No, wait, I think I've got a box of matches somewhere,' said Tad. He started searching his pockets.

At that moment, they all heard something. It was a strange rustling sound. It was like the sound of hundreds of dry leaves being stirred by the wind, and it seemed very close.

'What is that?' gasped Tamara.

'I'm not sure,' said Tad. 'But whatever it is, I don't much like it.' He had got the matches out now and was trying to fumble one of them from the box.

'Sounds to me like the kind of noise you'd associate with a large invertebrate,' said Tamara.

'A what?' muttered Jade.

'I mean a big—' Tamara stopped talking. She was staring at Tad. Rose followed her gaze and saw that something big and dark was rising up from the floor behind Tad – a great, long shape that seemed to rise higher and higher until it was towering six feet above him. Jade too had her back turned to the shape and was totally unaware of its presence.

'What are you all staring at?' asked Tad irritably.

'There's something behind you,' whispered Rose.

Tad sneered.

'Yeah, don't tell me, it's the Boogie Man. You know, kid, I'm getting a little bit tired of your fantasies.'

'It's not a fantasy,' said Tamara, her voice filled with dread. 'There really *is* something behind you.'

Tad grunted and struck a match. In the sudden glow, Rose could see exactly what was behind him. It was the biggest snake she had ever seen; a long glittering body covered in tiny scales and a great oval head from which two cold eyes stared down mercilessly. As she watched, horrified, the beast opened its jaws revealing huge fangs that dripped liquid and a forked tongue that flicked rapidly in and out.

Jade turned and looked at what was behind Tad. 'Well I think I'll be off now,' she said, and without another word, she turned and headed for the door as fast as her legs would carry her.

'Hey, where do you think you're going?' yelled Tad. 'We need to—'

Suddenly, shockingly, the snake shot downwards and its open jaws engulfed Tad's head and shoulders cutting off the rest of his sentence. He stood there for an instant, his body shuddering, the match still burning in his outstretched fingers.

'Tad!' Tamara opened her mouth and screamed. Then the match went out and there were just the awful sounds of slithering in the darkness.

Rose grabbed Tamara's hand and pulled her towards the door.

'Come on,' she said.

'Wait!' yelled Tamara. 'We can't just leave him.'

'We have to,' said Rose. 'Don't you see, it's his turn. These films are always like this. We have to get out of here or we'll be next.'

She dragged Tamara from the room and slammed the door behind them. They turned to run along the corridor beyond. Halfway along it, they saw two figures grappling in a patch of moonlight. Jade was struggling with a big muscular figure, a creature that looked more like an ape than a man.

'What the hell is that?' shrieked Tamara.

'It's a Number Tail,' said Rose grimly.

As they drew closer, they saw that the creature was in the act of biting a large chunk out of Jade's neck and judging by the noise she was making, she wasn't enjoying the experience much.

Tamara looked frantically around for a weapon and spotted a red fire-extinguisher fixed to one wall. She wrenched it from its mounting and brought it down on the ape-like creature's head. He sprawled on the floor and didn't get up again. Tamara dropped the extinguisher and kneeled to look at Jade, but it was clear at a glance that she was badly injured. Blood was pumping from the wound on her neck, soaking into her T-shirt.

'What...was that thing?' she croaked.

'It was a...' Tamara looked at Rose.

'A Number Tail.'

'What's that?' gasped Jade.

'Never mind,' said Tamara. She took hold of one of Jade's hands and tried to help her to her feet, but she shook her head.

'No use,' she croaked. 'I'm...done for, I'm afraid. Leave me and...save yourselves.'

'But—'

'Go,' she groaned. 'I think there may be...more of them. They must have...made their home up here...I think this is their...lair.'

Rose turned her head as she heard sounds coming from the corridor behind her. Other Neanderthals were shambling out of dark doorways. Beams of moonlight were spilling in through a line of barred windows and she caught glimpses of long hair, huge foreheads and bared teeth. The creatures turned towards her and started lurching along the corridor.

'Tamara!' she squealed.

Tamara glanced up, took one look and then jumped to her feet.

'Come on,' she yelled, and she and Rose ran along the corridor, leaving Jade to her fate. Rose glanced

173

back and saw that the creatures were closing in on her. In an instant she was buried beneath an onslaught of hungry cavemen and her screams echoed along the corridor.

'Look!' Tamara pointed. At the top of the corridor, another flight of stairs angled upwards. They ran towards them and went up as fast as their legs would carry them.

There was a sudden flash of blinding light and Mr Lazarus had to shield his eyes from the glare. The wooden platform slid smoothly forward and there was Captain Holder, standing on the platform, a look of complete shock on his grizzled features. He was holding a torch in one hand and the Retriever in the other, blinking around at his surroundings.

'What the hell is going on?' he demanded. He noticed Mr Lazarus standing there and gave him a challenging look. 'Who the hell are you?' he said. 'And where the hell am I?'

Mr Lazarus sighed wearily. This exercise was turning out to be a whole lot more complicated than he had anticipated. He lifted his hands in a gesture of surrender.

'Don't worry, Captain Holder,' he said. 'I can assure you, I'm on your side.'

'Yeah? Well, perhaps you'd like to tell me what's going on here? And how you know my name.'

Mr Lazarus smiled.

'I'll certainly give it my best shot,' he said.

Kip and Beth raced up the staircase to the first floor, horribly aware that the sabre-toothed tiger was coming after them in hot pursuit and gaining on them by the second. Beth was still holding the machete; it wasn't much but it was the only weapon they had. Glancing back, Kip saw that the tiger was only a few feet behind Beth's racing heels, and he realised that they would have to turn back and try to fight the beast.

Just then, a figure appeared on the stairs ahead of him – a big bare-chested Neanderthal. The creature was holding a spear and had a look of absolute rage on his ugly features. He lifted the spear with a bellow of defiance and came racing down the stairs towards Kip, who stopped dead in his tracks. Beth crashed into him and knocked him over. They went down in a sprawl, and the machete fell from Beth's hand and clattered down the stairs. The Neanderthal was almost upon them. Kip gritted his teeth, anticipating the thrust of the spear but inexplicably, the Neanderthal raced straight by him and Beth, as though they were of no interest to him whatsoever. For an instant, Kip was bewildered but a ferocious roar made him snap his gaze round to look back down the stairs. The Neanderthal had plunged the spear into the chest of the tiger and now the animal was roaring and lashing out with its paws as the Neanderthal attempted to push it back down the stairs.

A moment later, two more armed Neanderthals appeared on the landing and ran down to the first one's assistance. As they raced past Kip, he realised what was happening. This must be the Neanderthal's lair. They were simply defending it against one of their deadliest enemies. Clearly dinner could wait until they'd managed to drive off the tiger.

'Come on, let's keep going,' he gasped, disentangling himself from Beth. They got to their feet and looked back at the battle that was going on below them. The Neanderthals had formed a barrier and were moving slowly down the stairs, jabbing at the tiger with their spears. The tiger wasn't at all happy with the situation. It was roaring and thrashing its tail, but it was slowly being driven backwards.

Without another word, Kip grabbed Beth's hand and pulled her up the staircase. 'We've got to find the room with the incubators,' he yelled.

'What?' asked Beth.

'It's where the Retriever is,' Kip reminded her. They reached the landing and turned into the corridor beyond. Kip ducked his head into one empty room and shone the flashlight inside it. What he saw in there startled him. Crouched in the corners of the room were groups of Neanderthal women and children, who shrieked and held their hands up to their eyes as the torch beam dazzled them.

'Oops. Sorry!' he said and moved quickly on. He tried the next room. Empty. He ran on again and came to a closed door. In the light of the torch he saw a couple of words stencilled on the door. *Incubation Room*.

'This has to be it,' he said. He opened the door and shone the torch inside.

'Let me get this straight,' growled Captain Holder. He was sitting on the platform now, his head in his hands. 'You're saying I'm just a character in a movie?'

'Yes,' said Mr Lazarus. 'That is correct. Oh, in another life you are the famous movie actor, Clint Westwood. But in *this* life you are, forgive me for saying this, just a work of fiction.'

'But that's ridiculous,' snarled Captain Holder. 'I'm a ship's captain. I've worked on boats since I was a teenager.'

'No, that's just the part you're playing,' said Mr Lazarus. He thought for a moment. 'Look,' he said, 'let's just try something.' He walked across the projection room and rummaged around on a workbench. Eventually he found a length of rope. He came back and handed it to Captain Holder. 'Now, if you really have spent your life on the ocean, you'll be able to do a running bowline for me.'

'A running *what*?'

'A bowline. It's just about the most-used knot on any ship you care to mention. Any sailor worth his salt will know how to tie one.'

'Oh, OK.' Captain Holder took the rope in his hands and stared at it for several moments. He actually started to try and tie a knot but after a few moments, he shook his head. 'Nope,' he said. 'Haven't a clue.'

'All right then. How about a rolling hitch? Or a sheet bend?'

Captain Holder stared at him.

'Sounds like you're talking a foreign language,' he admitted.

'Well, I ask you. How likely is that? I know how to do those knots because I used to work at a cinema in Venice and all my equipment had to be carried to and from it by boat. But you, supposedly a captain for many years, can't even come close to doing it. And yet,' he pointed to the projector, 'What can you tell me about that?'

Captain Holder smiled. 'Say, that's an old Westar, isn't it?' he said. 'Haven't seen one of those babies in a very long time. Must date from the—' He paused, looked surprised. 'Now, how in the hell would I know that?' he muttered.

'Because you . . . or rather, your other self . . . has spent a lifetime working in the movies. Projection equipment is something you would be very familiar with.'

Captain Holder frowned.

'I guess that does make some kind of sense,' he agreed. 'That spooky little girl who turned up on the boat, she kept saying, over and over, that we were in some kind of movie. But it sure *felt* real.' He shrugged, shook his head. 'Anyway, Mr Lassoo, or whatever your name is, I guess I should thank you for pulling me out of there. It was getting pretty hairy, to tell you the truth. Now if you'll just show me the way out of this place, I'll get out of your way.'

Mr Lazarus was horrified.

'Oh, no, no, you can't stay here! You don't belong in this world. Forgive me, I don't mean to sound rude, but you must go back into the film.'

'Are you kidding me? Go back into that hellhole? Call me old-fashioned, but that's not my idea of a good time.'

'I appreciate that but *think* for a moment! We know you're not really a captain, but in the movie you are, and a captain always takes responsibility for everyone in his care, right?'

Captain Holder frowned. 'I guess,' he said, but he didn't sound convinced.

'Well then, the remaining members of your crew are depending on you to get them out of trouble.'

'What do you mean the *remaining* members. Are you saying...?'

'Since you've been gone, several of them have...' – Mr Lazarus searched for the right way to say it – '...expired.'

Captain Holder looked shocked.

'I've only been gone a few minutes,' he protested.

'I know. And that's exactly the problem. They didn't have your guiding hand to steer them out of trouble.'

'What happened to them?'

Mr Lazarus frowned.

'Well, it's been rather difficult to follow,' said Mr Lazarus. 'What's the young man called? Todd?'

'Tad.'

'Yes. He's been swallowed by a giant snake.'

Captain Holder stared at him. 'Are you kidding me?'

'I would never joke about such things. And the younger woman...Jade? I believe she was just eaten by Neanderthals.'

'By what?'

'Cavemen. Cannibalistic cavemen. There's only Doctor Flyte and Rose left and they are depending on you to come back and save them.'

'I see.' Captain Holder still didn't seem entirely

convinced. 'That's all very well but, like I said, it's hairy in there. I could die.'

'Oh, that's not going to happen!' Mr Lazarus gave a dismissive laugh. 'This movie is a big hit. They're talking sequels. They're talking a three-movie deal. Naturally they'll want you back for part two.' Mr Lazarus was making it up as he went along, but he could see that he had Captain Holder's interest.

'Hmm. What's the second movie about?'

'The scriptwriters are still working on the storyline . . . but I believe in that one you have the lead role. In fact, they are building the entire picture around you.'

'Really?' Captain Holder looked more interested now. He seemed to consider for a moment. 'And you said that Doctor Flyte hasn't been harmed?'

'Not yet,' admitted Mr Lazarus. 'But she's in a very . . . what did you call it? A very hairy situation.' He looked at Captain Holder slyly. 'I think you like Doctor Flyte, don't you?' he said.

'She's OK,' admitted Captain Holder. 'For a dame.'

'Hmm. And what if I told you that she's very attracted to you?'

'Me? Hell, no. If she is, she's pretty good at keeping it hidden.'

'Oh, that's just her way. But I overheard her talking to Jade. This was before she was killed by the Neanderthals . . .'

'Obviously.'

'She was telling Jade how much she admired you...your strength, your courage, your...rugged good looks.'

'She said that?' Captain Holder smiled. 'Hey, how about that?' He seemed to consider for a moment. 'I guess you're right,' he said. 'A good captain never deserts his crew, huh?'

'Absolutely,' said Mr Lazarus and he gave a smart salute. 'Good to have you back on board, Captain!'

'OK, so I'm convinced. How do I get back in there?'

'No, wait just a minute. A couple of things. First, that torch you're carrying? Hang onto it very tightly when I send you back. The Neanderthals spend most of their time in darkness. If you shine that into their faces I believe it will dazzle them.'

'This?' Captain Holder stared at it. 'It's just an ordinary torch.'

'Even so. Trust me. And the thing you have in your other hand? Don't press the button again, whatever you do. Close the metal cover. Yes, that's the way! I want you to give the device to a boy called Kip.'

'Who the hell is Kip?'

'He's a friend of mine. I sent him into the film to bring back his little sister. The weird girl you mentioned?'

'And how the hell did *she* get in there?'

'Too long a story, I'm afraid. And we're too near the end of the film to waste any more time. You'd better prepare yourself.'

'OK.' Captain Holder climbed back onto the platform. 'I'm ready,' he said.

'Excellent. Oh and, Captain Holder?'

'Yes?'

'Please try not to say "hell" so much. It's not very polite.'

'OK, pal, whatever you say.' Captain Holder adopted a macho pose. 'Let's get this show on the road,' he yelled. 'GERONIMO!'

And with that, Mr Lazarus kicked the platform back into the light.

CHAPTER SEVENTEEN
ON THE ROOF

Rose and Tamara raced full pelt up the gloomy staircase, pursued by several hungry Neanderthals. They reached the third-floor landing and stood there for a moment, glancing hopelessly around. Rose noticed another short flight of stairs and a stencilled sign that read, TO THE ROOF.

'Come on!' she screamed and pulled Tamara after her.

'But we'll be trapped up there,' gasped Tamara.

Rose glanced desperately back the way they had come. A group of shambling, ragged figures were bounding up the stairs after them and there was simply no other place to go. They made it to the short flight of stone steps and went up them, as fast as they could. The door at the top of the steps was ajar. They burst through it and found themselves on a wide stretch of flat roof. A full moon sent a wash of silvery light over its concrete surface. As far as they could see, there were no Neanderthals up here.

They turned back to the door and swung it shut, but it was flimsy with age and they both realised it could not hold back the cavemen for very long.

Even as they threw their weight against it, they felt the ancient wood shuddering and buckling under the impact of several pounding fists. Tamara snatched up a length of wood lying by the doorway and pushed it though the door's metal hasp. Then she and Rose backed slowly away, staring fearfully at the door, seeing how the length of wood was already bending beneath the pressure of so many hands.

Tamara ran to the edge of the roof and peered down into the darkness. It was too high to jump and there was no sign of any way they might climb down. They turned back to face the door as a loud splintering sound filled the night air. The length of wood had just snapped in two and now the first of the creatures was emerging onto the roof.

Tamara threw her arms around Rose and pulled her close. 'Shut your eyes, honey,' she whispered. 'It'll soon be over.'

They waited for the end, all hope gone.

And then they heard a noise from above them – the droning, rhythmic sound of an engine. Rose looked up in amazement. Something was hovering in the air thirty feet above them, lights flashing on its metal fuselage. *A helicopter!* As she stared at it in amazement, a hatch opened and a rope ladder began to descend towards them.

★

At first, Kip wasn't sure what he was looking at. The light of the torch picked out a great mass of shifting coils over in one corner of the room. Then something reared up from the midst of them, a huge oval head with two staring eyes, and he began to understand what it was. It was some kind of prehistoric snake; the biggest reptile he had ever seen. This would have been bad enough but sticking out from the snake's mouth was a pair of human legs – legs that kicked desperately as they slid, bit by bit, down the snake's gullet. For a horrible moment, Kip thought they might be Rose's legs, but then he reasoned that Rose didn't own a pair of heavy boots like the ones he was looking at. *One of the men from the film*, he told himself. *Most probably Tad Baxter. He was now lowest down the cast list.*

He swept the torch beam around the rest of the room and saw the glass tanks Mr Lazarus had mentioned, but there was no sign of the Retriever in any of them and he certainly didn't feel much like going in there and doing a more thorough search. A slithering sound from the far corner made him snap the beam back in that direction, only to see that the snake had finished ingesting its dinner and was now moving in his direction. He cursed and slammed the door.

'Wasn't it in there?' asked Beth. 'That has to be the room.'

'Take it from me,' said Kip. 'You don't want to go in there.'

'But we have to,' argued Beth. 'We can't get back without the Retriever.' She went to open the door again but Kip put a hand on her arm.

'Trust me,' he said. 'Don't go in there.'

Just then Mr Lazarus's voice buzzed in his ear.

'Kip, are you OK?'

'No I'm not. The bloody Retriever's not here!'

'I know.' Mr Lazarus sounded annoyingly calm. 'And there's absolutely no need for bad language. It arrived back here a few minutes ago, but I've just sent it into the film again.'

'This is getting ridiculous,' complained Kip. 'Where is the pigging thing? It's like a flipping yo-yo.'

'Don't worry about that. Just concentrate on finding Rose.'

'That's easy for you to say,' screamed Kip. 'You're not stuck in this madhouse. Now just tell me where—'

'She's on the ruh–' The Communicator gave a loud beep and went silent. Kip stared down at it in dismay. He pulled it out of the holster and thumped it a couple of times, but it was as dead as a doornail.

'Oh, brilliant,' said Kip. 'It's packed up.'

Beth was staring at him in open-mouthed dismay. 'Now what do we do?' she asked.

Kip shook his head.

'I have no idea,' he said. 'Rose is on the *ruh*.'

'The what?'

'The *ruh!* That's all I heard before the pigging phone conked out.'

Beth thought for a moment. 'The . . . *railway?*' she suggested. 'The . . . *racecourse?*'

'What are you babbling about?' cried Kip.

'I'm trying to think of things that begin with *ruh*.'

'Oh, and you reckon there's a railway around here, do you?' Kip shook his head. 'And a racecourse!' he yelled. 'That's really likely, isn't it? What are we going to do now?'

'I tell you what we're going to do,' said Beth quietly. 'We're going to run.' She was pointing back along the corridor. Kip turned his head to look and saw that a couple of Neanderthals had just come round the corner from the direction of the lower staircase. They were all scratched and bloody from their fight with the sabre-toothed tiger, and the ends of their spears glistened with gore. Clearly the third member of their party was either dead or incapable of walking. Now they were staring at the two friends and the expressions on their faces were far from welcoming.

'Good idea,' said Kip and he turned and led the way along the corridor. They reached the end and found another staircase leading up. They made it to the next landing without trouble, but glancing back Kip could see that the two Neanderthals were climbing up after them. Kip shone his torch frantically around to try and get his bearings. Ahead of him was a short flight of stone steps and at the top of it, several Neanderthals were banging their fists against a closed door, a door that even as Kip watched was beginning to shatter under the onslaught of those powerful fists. On the wall beside them was a sign that read TO THE ROOF.

'*RUH!*' yelled Beth, pointing.

'Huh?' Kip stared at her, thinking that she must have lost her mind.

'The roof, you idiot! That must be where Rose is.'

'Oh right,' said Kip. He was going to say something else but an angry bellow from just behind him made him spin round. The two armed Neanderthals had just come round the corner and were racing towards him, their spears raised to strike. But in turning, Kip had accidentally pointed the torch in their direction, directing the beam full into their faces. The effect was astonishing. The two Neanderthals dropped their spears and lifted their hands to shield their eyes. They screamed in absolute terror.

Kip stared at them in amazement.

'The torches,' he gasped. 'They can't take the light. It dazzles them.'

'They'll soon get used to it,' Beth told him.

'Never mind.' Kip put a hand on Beth's shoulder and turned her round. He pointed at the bunch of cavemen at the top of the short flight of stairs. What was left of the door was breaking and splintering beneath their combined attack. 'We've got to get through them,' he said. 'We'll use the torches.'

'But . . . they're facing away from us!'

'Then we've got to get their attention, somehow. What did Mr Lazarus say distracted them? Opera? Do you know any opera?'

If Beth did, she wasn't about to admit it.

'Beth, what songs do you know?' yelled Kip. He was keeping his light trained on the two armed Neanderthals, who were cowering away from the light as though it was burning them. 'You need to sing something.'

She glanced at him in sheer disbelief.

'What do you think this is?' she asked him. 'The X Factor?'

'Never mind that. Just sing something. Anything.'

'You *are* kidding, I hope.'

'No, I'm *not* kidding,' bellowed Kip. He pointed to the creatures on the stairs. 'Sing to them, *loudly*. They're nearly through that door and I think Rose is on the other side of it. We've got to try and get them to turn round.'

'I don't believe this,' protested Beth.

'Just do it,' pleaded Kip. 'Please! There can't be much time left. The film's nearly over. If we get to the credits, we're all stuck here for ever!'

Beth looked at him in alarm. Then her shoulders slumped and she moved to the foot of the steps.

'What do you want me to sing?' she asked.

'I don't care. The first thing that comes into your head. Just sing something!'

She nodded. She cleared her throat and she began to sing as loudly as she could. Her voice seemed to echo in the narrow confines of the landing.

'Half a pound of tuppeny rice . . .'

Ape-like heads turned to stare at her in dull surprise.

'. . . half a pound of treacle . . .'

More heads at the back of the queue turned and Beth gave them a blast of torchlight full in the face. Two Neanderthals screamed, lost their footing and fell down the steps onto the concrete floor below. Emboldened, Beth moved closer.

'That's the way the money goes . . .'

More of the creatures were turning round to see where the sound was coming from and as they did, each of them received the torch treatment.

'It's working!' gasped Kip. 'Keep singing.'

'Pop goes the weasel!'

The two of them began to advance up the steps, Beth at the front, still singing and still blasting

191

Neanderthals, Kip fighting a deadly rearguard action on the half-blinded creatures that were stumbling in pursuit. On either side of them, screaming Neanderthals fell down the steps, groping blindly as they went. Within a matter of moments Kip and Beth had cleared a path to the doorway but they could see that several of the creatures had already made it through onto the roof. They had no other choice but to follow.

Kip gritted his teeth, hoping against hope that they wouldn't be too late.

Rose stared up at the slowly descending ladder. An amplified American-accented voice rang from the hovering helicopter.

'Hold tight, we'll get you out of there just as soon as we can. We picked up your distress signal and came looking for you. We were just about to give up and head back to base.'

Rose looked hopefully at Tamara but saw that she was staring towards the doorway where several Neanderthals were coming slowly across the flat roof towards them, their powerful arms extended. Rose looked anxiously back towards the helicopter. The rope ladder was descending, but slowly, much too slowly for comfort, and the leading Neanderthals were already very close.

'Hurry up!' yelled Rose. 'There's not much time.'

Tamara was looking around for some kind of weapon but there was nothing here she might be able to use. She seemed to come to a decision. She let go of Rose's hand and stepped forward to face the first Neanderthal.

'OK, you big ape,' she said. 'You want trouble, you came to the right place.'

'Tamara, no!' cried Rose. 'Come back here.'

'It's OK, honey. I'm just going to buy us a little more time. Don't worry, I'm a black belt in karate.' She launched herself forward and aimed a savage kick into the creature's groin. He gave a small grunt of surprise, but didn't seem hurt in any way. Now Tamara threw a punch at his stomach. He grunted again, but didn't seem particularly bothered. Now it was his turn. He reached out a dirty hand, grabbed a fistful of Tamara's hair and flung her to the ground. She hit the roof with a thud and rolled over. The Neanderthal stepped closer and reaching down, he grabbed Tamara by the arm and pulled her upright. Then he began to strangle her.

'NO!' screamed Rose. 'Please. Let her go!'

She started forward to try and help but froze in her tracks as she heard a sudden whooshing noise. There was a brilliant flash of light. Quite suddenly, Captain Holder was standing beside her, looking somewhat bewildered. He was holding a torch.

He looked down at Rose and smiled with what looked like relief.

'I'm back,' he said. 'I'm really back!'

'Never mind that!' screamed Rose. 'Help her!' She pointed to where Tamara and the Neanderthal were struggling together. Captain Holder said something under his breath and sprang towards them. He drew back his fist and punched the Neanderthal full in the face. The caveman's head rocked a little but he seemed completely undeterred. Then Captain Holder appeared to remember something. He flicked the torch on and brought it up to point the beam right into the creature's eyes.

The result was amazing. The Neanderthal bellowed as though in terrible pain. He let go of Tamara and, lifting his hands to his face, he tried to stumble away, unaware that he was moving towards the edge of the roof. One of his feet stepped out onto empty air and he stood there a moment, waving his arms in a pathetic attempt to stay upright. Then he fell.

Rose ran to Tamara who was clutching her throat and gasping for breath.

'Are you all right?' she asked.

Tamara nodded her head. She looked at Captain Holder. 'Where have you been?' she croaked.

'You wouldn't believe me if I told you,' he said. 'Are you two OK?'

Tamara nodded grimly. More Neanderthals were approaching and Captain Holder swung round and gave them a blast from his torch to slow them down. He glanced up at the helicopter and saw that the rope ladder was finally coming within reach.

'Who are these people?' he asked suspiciously.

'I don't care who they are,' said Tamara, getting to her feet. 'So long as they're human and they've used a bar of soap in the last six months, then they've got my vote.'

'OK, Tamara,' said Captain Holder. He did something odd then. He reached out and took her in his arms, staring longingly into her eyes. 'You knew I'd come back for you, didn't you?' he said, and his voice sounded less gruff than usual.

Tamara stared at him, a little bewildered.

'I . . . kind of *hoped* you would,' she admitted.

'I guess you were depending on my strength, my courage, my rugged good looks.' He leaned closer, going in for a kiss.

'Er . . . could we talk about this later?' asked Tamara. 'Only it's a little frantic right now.'

'Oh sure.' Captain Holder seemed to remember where they were. 'No problem. You go first. Then the girl.'

Tamara nodded. She threw up a hand and grabbed the bottommost rung of the rope ladder. Rose could see the highly-defined muscles in her arm flexing. She clambered up a short distance and then reached a hand down to Rose.

'Come on, honey,' she said. 'Let's get out of here.'

Rose reached up to grab Tamara's hand. She scrambled onto the bottom rung of the rope ladder; but just then, she heard somebody shout her name. Turning, she saw that two figures had just emerged from the shattered doorway and were running frantically towards the helicopter, weaving in and out of the slower-moving Neanderthals. Rose gasped in surprise. Kip and Beth. She stared down at them amazed.

'What are *you* doing here?'

'We came to get you,' yelled Kip, having to shout over the roar of the helicopter's rotor blades. Beth turned to train her torch on the advancing Neanderthals and Captain Holder went to assist her. 'We've been following you all through this pigging film,' added Kip, gazing up at her. 'You won't believe what we've had to go through to get here.'

Rose scowled down at him.

'Well, you needn't have bothered,' she said. 'I'm going off with Tamara now.'

'You're *what*?' Kip stared at her, horrified. 'You...you can't!' he protested. 'If you do that, you'll be stuck in the film. You'll never be able to get out of it.'

'Tamara's my friend,' said Rose. 'She's looked after

me, really, really well, which is more than you ever did.'

'That...that's not fair,' said Kip. He paced anxiously around on the roof for a few moments. 'And anyway, what about Mum and Dad?'

'What about them?' muttered Rose. 'Tamara is pretty and she has Barbie-doll hair and she nearly got killed trying to look after me.'

Tamara was looking intently down at Rose now and her eyes filled with tears.

'Honey, if you have a Mommy and Daddy waiting for you, maybe you should go with...' She glared down at Kip. 'Who are you exactly?'

'I'm her brother.'

'Yes, he's my brother,' said Rose. 'And he's always being mean to me. He makes nasty comments when I play with my dolls and he makes me sit up in the projection room when he wants to go in and watch a film.'

'I won't do that to you again,' Kip told her. 'I promise. And I won't make comments about your dolls any more. OK? Rose, you're my sister and I...well, I...' He made a real effort to get the words out. 'I...*care* about you,' he said. 'Lots.'

Rose didn't look at all convinced.

'You're just saying that,' she sneered. 'You're just worried what Mum and Dad will say if you go back without me.'

Kip looked up at her desperately. Now the helicopter was starting to rise higher in the air.

'Rose, you've *got* to come back with me. You're not meant to be here, none of us are. And if we don't go very soon, it will be too late for all of us. Do you want to be stuck here for the rest of your life? Being chased by smelly cavemen.'

'Well . . .' said Rose.

'Please, just let go of the ladder and I'll catch you.' He shoved his torch into his pocket and held out his hands. 'Just let go.'

'You'll drop me,' cried Rose.

'I won't, I promise. Come on, it's only a short distance.'

Rose frowned. She looked up at Tamara and sighed.

'I suppose I'll *have* to go with him,' she said.

'OK, honey.' Tamara leaned down and gave Rose a kiss on the cheek. 'It was sure nice meeting you. And I'll never forget you.'

Rose smiled. She glanced down again. 'Don't you dare drop me,' she warned Kip.

'I won't.'

Rose took a deep breath. Then she let go of Tamara's hand and fell the short distance into Kip's arms. He held her close to him and she hugged him back.

'I was so frightened,' she whispered into his ear.

'A big snake ate Tad. And Jade got killed by Number Tails.'

'It's not real,' Kip assured her.

'It *felt* real,' said Rose.

'Well, you're safe now,' he said. 'I've got you.'

'Are we going home now?'

'Yes,' said Kip. 'We—' But then a sudden terrible thought struck him. 'Oh no,' he gasped, 'the Retriever!' He looked at Beth. 'We still don't have the Retriever. We can't get back without it.'

A big hand came to rest on his shoulder and he looked up in surprise to see Captain Holder smiling at him.

'I guess you must be Kip,' he said.

Kip nodded, mystified.

'A crazy old guy asked me to give you this.' Captain Holder reached into the pocket of his leather jacket and pulled out the Retriever. 'He said you'd know what to do with it.' He pressed it into Kip's hand. 'Well, I'd love to stand around and chew the fat but it's time I made a move.'

He threw his torch at the head of the nearest Neanderthal, then made a quick run across the intervening space and launched himself through the air in what could only be described as a heroic leap. His hands slapped around the bottom rung of the rope ladder. He clung on and waved his arm at the helicopter pilot. The rope ladder began to glide slowly back up into the helicopter. At the same time, it swung away from the rooftop, taking Tamara and Captain Holder with it. For a few moments, the pair of them were still visible, waving down at the three children on the roof, but then they were gone, swallowed up by the darkness. Only the blinking red lights of the helicopter revealed where they were.

'Right,' said Kip. He set Rose down on the roof and hung the Retriever around his neck. Beth was still dazzling Neanderthals for all she was worth, but it was clear that it was a losing battle. The creatures were blundering closer and closer all the time, their eyes gradually adjusting to the glare, their arms groping to try and touch what they wanted more than anything else. Fresh meat. More and more of them were spilling out onto the roof through the shattered doorway.

'Everybody hold hands,' instructed Kip. 'We'd better hurry, we must be really close to the end credits.'

Beth dropped her torch and did as she was told. Kip was painfully aware of the Neanderthals, unhindered now, closing in for the kill on all sides. He glanced around at the other's anxious faces. 'Everybody hang on tight,' he warned them. He let go of Beth's hand for one second, levered up the cover on the Retriever and pressed the EXIT button. Then instantly, he grabbed her hand again.

For a long, terrible moment, nothing happened. Absolutely nothing. Kip stared down at the Retriever for a moment and glanced nervously over his shoulder, only to see a hideous bearded figure closing in on him with an expression of feral rage. He saw two red, staring eyes, two rows of rotten teeth and two big hands with dirty fingernails. He was so scared, he nearly let go of Beth and Rose so he could make a run for it. But he hung on tightly.

Then the familiar melting sensation pulsed through him and he was only dimly aware of the Neanderthal's hands passing right through him as though he had no more substance than a shadow. A bright light flared with a brilliance that momentarily blinded him . . . and, an instant later, he was standing on the wooden platform as it slid smoothly out of the light.

CHAPTER EIGHTEEN
THE RETURN

Kip blinked a couple of times and let his vision swim back into focus. He was relieved to see that Beth and Rose were also there, crammed together on the round wooden platform. Then he turned his head and saw Mr Lazarus, a welcoming smile on his face.

'So you're back at last,' he said. 'I was beginning to fear you'd left it too late. That you were going to end up like Federico.' He gestured to the glass window and Kip could see the end credits going up the screen, the final theme music playing. 'You made it out of there by the skin of your teeth,' he said.

Kip let go of Beth and Rose's hands and stepped off the platform. They followed, all of them staring around, as though trying to convince themselves that they really were back in the projection room of the Paramount.

'That was very nearly an unhappy ending,' Kip told Mr Lazarus. 'When we finally got to Rose, she was just about to go off with Kara Neetly in a helicopter.'

Rose shook her head.

'Her name was Tamara Flyte,' she said. 'And she was an anthro . . . an anthro . . . she was a nice lady.'

'Yes, she seemed very nice,' said Mr Lazarus. 'And she looked after you well.' He smiled at Kip. 'I saw the last scene, by the way. It was very emotional.'

Kip shrugged his shoulders. He glanced at Beth. 'Are you OK?' he asked her.

She nodded. 'That was beyond weird,' she said.

'It was 'orrible,' whispered Rose. 'There was snakes and Number Tails and all kinds of nasty things. Just wait till I tell Mummy and Daddy what happened.'

'You don't need to tell them,' said Beth anxiously. 'Do you?'

'Yes I do.'

Kip fixed Mr Lazarus with a look and lowered his voice to a whisper. 'What are we going to do about Rose?' he asked.

Mr Lazarus smiled.

'*Do* about her?' he echoed.

'She'll tell everyone what happened. Anyone who'll listen. She won't be able to stop herself.'

'And you think people will believe her?'

Kip shrugged.

'They might if she goes on about it enough.'

Mr Lazarus considered for a moment. Then he nodded.

'Rose, come here,' he said. 'I have something to show you.' He pulled an old-fashioned pocket watch from his waistcoat. It looked just like the one he had given to Norman. 'Now, look at this for a moment,' he said. He let it dangle from its length of chain and began to swing it gently from side to side. 'If you look really closely,' he said, 'you'll see a little dancing pony.'

Rose fixed her gaze on the watch and Kip noticed Mr Lazarus's lips moving as though he was chanting something under his breath. Suddenly, Rose's eyelids fluttered and she began to fall. Kip caught her under her arms and looked at her pale face in dismay.

'What's wrong with her?' he gasped.

'Nothing,' Mr Lazarus assured him. 'She'll sleep now and when she wakes up she'll remember hardly anything about her experience. If she should ask any questions, just tell her it must have been a nightmare she had.'

Kip nodded. He lifted Rose into his arms and carried her across to the folding bed on the far side of the room. She was clearly in a deep sleep but her chest rose and fell and there was a smile on her face, as though she was having a nice dream.

Only now that he was out of the film, could Kip fully appreciate what he had been through. He lifted a hand to his face and rubbed at his eyes.

'You must be exhausted,' observed Mr Lazarus. 'After all, it's not every day you take on Neanderthals and sabre-toothed tigers.'

'And a giant bat,' said Beth. 'I expect you missed that bit.'

Mr Lazarus nodded. 'I didn't see *everything*,' he admitted. 'Most of the time I was following the action with Rose. But I did see you arrive on the roof. That was quite a scene.' He smiled. 'I think we should all head outside now,' he added. 'If I'm correct, your father will be arriving back any moment. Let's hope he doesn't notice how grubby you all are.'

'Dad!' Kip had forgotten all about his father's trip to the hospital. He glanced at Beth. 'We have to act like it's just been a normal night at the Paramount,' he warned her.

Beth was looking down at her torn T-shirt and stained jeans.

'Don't worry, I wasn't planning on telling anyone the truth,' she said. 'Though how I'm going to explain this lot, I don't know. These jeans were clean on today.'

'I think you three need to get a good night's sleep,' said Mr Lazarus. 'We can discuss what happened in more detail when you've had time to think it over.'

'Yes,' said Kip. 'Good idea.' He pointed to the Lazarus Enigma. 'As for that thing, you need to take it apart. Seriously. We can't risk having any more accidents like the one we had with Rose.'

Mr Lazarus smiled thinly.

'Like I say, let's discuss it later. If I dismantle the system, then we won't have the improved picture quality and sound. Two things that I think are already helping the cinema to find the wider audience it needs.'

'Well—' said Kip.

'No, come along now, no more discussion! Let's get you outside. We'll talk about this another time. And besides, we need to see the rest of the audience out.'

'The audience!' Kip opened his mouth in dismay. He'd forgotten all about them. He looked at Beth. 'What are they going to think?' he gasped. 'They must have seen everything!'

'They'll think they've seen a very bad film,' said Mr Lazarus calmly. 'One or two might even tell themselves that they've seen somebody they recognise in there. But who's going to believe what they say? That the boy who sells the popcorn and his friend were in a Hollywood movie?' He laughed. 'Who would believe such a ridiculous story? And if they should come back for another look, well, they'll see that they must have been mistaken. Because the film will be back the way it was always meant to be.'

Kip lifted Rose into his arms again and swung her carefully across his shoulder. She didn't stir. She seemed to be in the deepest sleep.

'You're sure she'll wake up?' he muttered.

Mr Lazarus nodded. 'Of course,' he said. 'Trust me, Kip. You worry too much. Everything is going to be fine.' He held out a gloved hand. 'But I think once again you have forgotten something, yes?'

Kip looked at him, puzzled, and then realised what he was talking about. He unslung the Retriever from around his neck and handed it over. Mr Lazarus slipped the device into his waistcoat pocket. Then Kip unbuckled the leather holster containing the Communicator and Mr Lazarus dropped it onto the workbench.

'That thing conked out,' Kip told him. 'At a very awkward moment.'

'I'll have a look at it,' Mr Lazarus replied. 'It probably needs a few adjustments. There now. All done. Come along, you two.'

They made their way down the stairs of the auditorium and out into the foyer. The last stragglers were wandering through the exit, many of them looking extremely confused. Kip overheard one guy telling his friend that *Terror Island* had to be the most ridiculous film he'd ever seen. What was all that stuff about the little girl? And what about that weird bit where everything went into reverse and then speeded up again?'

His friend nodded. He couldn't understand why *Nessun Dorma* had started playing really loudly during one sequence, drowning out all the dialogue. Who were those two kids who seemed to pop up out of nowhere right at the very end of the film?

And why did they look so maddeningly familiar? Kip made sure that his face was turned away as the two customers walked past him.

'So, what did you both think of the experience?' asked Mr Lazarus.

'Scary,' said Kip. 'Very scary.'

'And very emotional,' added Beth. 'You really felt like you were in it.'

'So it wasn't all bad news?'

'No,' murmured Beth. 'It was a real adventure. One that I'll never forget.'

They reached the exit doors and stepped out into the cool night air. Kip found himself glancing nervously up and down the darkened street.

'Relax,' said Mr Lazarus. 'There are no Neanderthals here. Unless you count *them*.' Across the road, a party of people waiting at a bus stop were staring at Kip and Beth open-mouthed. Clearly they had just watched the film.

'I wish they'd stop staring at us like that,' muttered Beth.

'I don't know,' said Kip. 'I think it's kind of cool. It's almost like we're movie stars now.'

'Yeah. For one night only,' said Beth.

Mr Lazarus looked at the two of them sternly. 'I hope it goes without saying, but I'll say it anyway. Tell nobody about your little adventure. If people like the ones across the road ask, "Wasn't that you in the film I watched last night?" tell them they must be crazy. This has to remain our secret.'

Headlights illuminated them suddenly and Dad's car moved quietly into the vacant parking spot in front of the cinema. He wound down the window and looked out at them.

'How's that for perfect timing?' he called to them. Dad did a double take. 'Good grief, Kip, you look *filthy*!' he exclaimed.

'Er…yeah, it was quite messy cleaning up tonight. A lot of…spilled popcorn. Beth gave me a hand.' Kip took the opportunity to change the subject. 'Rose fell asleep ages ago,' he said. 'I guess it *is* kind of late for her.'

'Pop her in the back seat,' suggested Dad. 'Beth, I'll drop you at your place on the way home.'

'Thanks, Mr McCall.' Beth opened the rear door and Kip laid his sister gently on the back seat, then slid in beside her.

'How's Grannie?' Kip asked as Beth walked around and climbed into the passenger seat.

'She's fine,' Dad told Kip. 'I managed to get a message to your mum. She came to the hospital and is staying on there a bit longer, just till your gran is properly settled.' He looked out at the smiling face of Mr Lazarus. 'Any problems tonight?' he asked.

Mr Lazarus shook his head. 'None at all. In fact, it was a great success. Very nearly a full house. I'll lock the takings in the safe for the night, before I er... head for home.'

'Thanks,' said Dad. 'I don't know what I'd have done without you.'

'My pleasure, Mr McCall. I hope you know that as far as the Paramount is concerned, I will do everything in my power to keep it going.' Mr Lazarus raised a gloved hand. 'Now, I'll say goodnight to you all.' He glanced at Kip and winked slyly. 'Sweet dreams,' he said. He walked back to the entrance and stepped inside, closing the door behind him.

Dad shook his head. 'You know, sometimes, you'd almost swear he *lives* in that cinema,' he said. He started up the engine and drove away. They travelled the short distance to Beth's house in silence and stopped outside. Beth opened the door and climbed out.

'Thanks, Mr McCall,' she said. 'Goodnight.'

Kip opened his door too.

'I'll just say goodbye,' he said and Dad gave him a meaningful look, but Kip ignored it and walked with Beth along her garden path to the door of her house. They stood there for a moment. It was a clear night, and a crescent moon sailed in a nearly starless sky, so different from the huge full moon and the millions of shimmering stars they had witnessed in the skies over Terror Island.

'That was... fantastic,' said Kip.

Beth nodded. 'I'll say. Think Rose will remember any of it?'

'I hope not,' said Kip. 'I don't want to be the one who has to explain everything to Mum and Dad.'

There was a long silence before Beth said, 'It *was* amazing though, wasn't it? I mean, it was so . . . *real*.'

Kip nodded. 'Like watching a great movie,' he said. 'Only better.'

'I was, like, terrified. But at the same time, it was kind of cool.' She thought for a moment. 'And, boy, did we kick Neanderthal butt!' They laughed.

'Of course, we can't ever do it again,' said Kip. 'It was way too dangerous.'

'I guess,' agreed Beth. 'Unless . . .'

Kip looked at her.

'Unless what?' he asked.

'Well, unless it was a film that wasn't so deadly. You know, a comedy, or something . . . ? A film where people don't get eaten.'

'We'll have to see what comes up,' said Kip. 'Let's sleep on it.'

Beth nudged him in the ribs. 'Hey, I don't know if they give Oscars to people who visit movies, but you should get one for that little speech you made on the roof. When you told Rose you cared about her, and all that?'

Kip smiled.

'That's because it's true,' he said.

Beth raised her eyebrows and gave him a disbelieving look.

He smiled. 'Sure she can be a pain, but you know what? I meant every word of it. What was it your mum likes to say? You don't know what you've got till it's gone? Well, for a minute there, it looked like she *was* gone and I didn't like the idea, not one little bit.'

Kip glanced at Dad's car, realising he was probably impatient to get home, but he wanted to linger just a moment more. He'd talk about the adventure with Beth tomorrow in the full daylight, but then it wouldn't seem quite so real. It would be like some dream he'd had. Right now, it was still almost close enough to touch.

'You were great, by the way. For a girl, I mean. You know, the way you handled yourself in there? When that Neanderthal was throttling me, the way you . . .' He made a slashing motion with one hand. 'Well, thanks, anyway.'

'No worries,' said Beth. She smiled. 'It's late. I'd better go in.' She leaned forward and gave him a light kiss on the cheek. He felt himself colouring up, but somehow couldn't stop himself from grinning with pleasure.

'See you tomorrow,' he said. He turned and walked down the path to the car. He climbed into the passenger seat beside Dad.

Dad gave him that knowing look.

'*Now* tell me she's not your girlfriend,' he said.

But Kip didn't say anything. He didn't care what Dad thought. He didn't care about anything. He had been to Terror Island and lived to tell the tale. Now he just felt absolutely exhausted.

He leaned back in his seat, closed his eyes and he was fast asleep by the time they reached home.

DEREK KEILTY

ILLUSTRATED BY JONNY DUDDLE

It's time for revenge!

Will Gallows, a young elfling sky cowboy, is riding
out on a dangerous quest. His mission? To bring
Noose Wormworx, the evil snake-bellied troll, to
justice. Noose is wanted for the murder of Will's
pa, and Will won't stop until he's got revenge!

'Wow, what a brilliant read.
Fresh and original – and very
funny too. This cowboy's
riding to an exciting new
frontier in fiction.'
Joseph Delaney, author of
The Spook's Apprentice

9781849392365 £5.99

The Absolutely True Diary of a Part-time INDIAN

SHERMAN ALEXIE

WINNER OF THE NATIONAL BOOK AWARD

'Son,' Mr P said, 'you're going to find more and more hope the farther and farther you walk away from this sad, sad, sad reservation.'

So Junior, who is already beaten up regularly for being a skinny kid in glasses, goes to the rich white school miles away. Now he's a target there as well. How he survives all this is an absolute shining must-read, and a triumph of the human spirit.

'Excellent in every way, poignant and really funny and heartwarming and honest and wise and smart.'
NEIL GAIMAN

81842708446 £5.99

THE grk BOOKS

When Timothy Malt finds a little white dog sitting outside his house and decides to adopt him, he little suspects what adventures he is signing up for. He flies a helicopter in Eastern Europe, exposes an international art thief in New York, and chases bank robbers through the jungles of Brazil!

WHIZZ ROUND THE WORLD WITH A GRK BOOK!

9781842703847   9781842705278   9781842705537   9781842705599

9781842706602   9781842706619   9781842709313

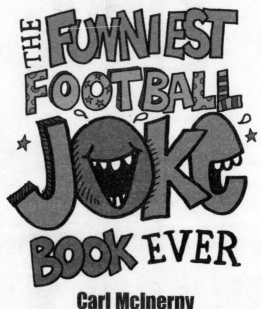

THE FUNNIEST FOOTBALL JOKE BOOK EVER

Carl McInerny

What will Fabio Capello do if the pitch is flooded during the World Cup? **Bring on his subs**

What did the ref say to the chicken who tripped a defender? **Fowl**

Why was the footballer upset on his birthday? **He got a red card**

These and many more howlers to make you laugh even if your team are losing!

781849391115 £3.99